Plenty of Freckles

By
Lisa VanderLeest

PublishAmerica
Baltimore

ISBN: 1-60441-827-3
PUBLISHED BY PUBLISHAMERICA, LLLP
www.publishamerica.com
Baltimore

Printed in the United States of America

To Mom and Dad

Bill and Carol Boyea

for all of their love and faith

1
A Vet's Life

When the storm came it wouldn't be any worse than the steady mist that was already icing its way under Jessie's windbreaker. Her footing slipped on a dash of ice along the country road she was walking and she cursed her feet for being so clumsy. It was a real Wisconsin winter; cold wet and loaded with slush.

The air she breathed was ominous and so thick it felt like she should swallow it in chunks instead of taking it into her lungs.

On the mile walk home from school she remembered, not long ago, when she was very young, that she had wished she was a pony and could gallop to and from school when the weather was bad.

Jessie smiled at the silly thought. Now that she was older she wished she had a snowmobile, or a bicycle, although she couldn't see how one of those would be any better than walking in this.

Almost there, she thought, knowing that if the weather was a hair worse she would have been met by her father or Max in one of the trucks; picked up and whisked away home.

Aunt Claudia had said this morning that a snow storm was indeed, on its way and it was fit to be a bad one. Her warning was the reason Jessie was wearing a windbreaker over her coat today. Aunt Claudia was wrong about some things but, not the weather. Oh, she could still wish that she had hooves and could canter out of this sloppy mess!

The wind was blowing her long black hair in her face and she dragged it back without a thought, revealing Irish blue eyes and a slight dusting of freckles on the bridge of her nose. These were fading as she grew up but, she had been called freckle face plenty of times because of them.

Her father said her freckles were just an 'Irish tradition'. Jessie only knew that she was going to miss them when they were gone. Things seemed to be an awful lot more simple when she was little. Growing up was kind of frightening and she wasn't sure she wanted to do it; even though it would give her more choices.

She wouldn't mind one bit if they moved away from Miller's Orchard. Now wasn't that just a tacky sort of name for town where she happened to be born? It wasn't even on the state map.

City life had to be more interesting than farm life but, her father would not even consider moving into town. She might as well get used to the idea that she was stuck here.

Someday she would be older. The decision would be hers. She knew she would miss her friends if she moved but, what was there look forward to when she went home now? The minute she reached home she would have to go right out and feed the cows. The only good part was the cows gave off an awful lot of warmth. She would be able to thaw a little bit before taking care of the chickens and Oh, E' gads!, their clucking and scratching would someday be enough to drive her mad!

Claudia Hicks had already remarked on the expression Jessie had used. 'Those chickens will drive me mad!'

"Mellow dramatics!" Aunt Claudia had laughed, teasingly. "Oh, Jessie, we would all be proud of you. Quite the little actress, I'll say! And with you already thirteen we should see a star in say...ten years, maybe less. Someday you should put it to use and make us all rich beyond our wildest dreams. Keep practicing. Then you can have your wish. We'd never have to work again; except for you, of course, dear. It would be one smashing performance after another."

'It just goes to show that it wasn't safe to complain about work in front of Aunt Claudia,' Jessie thought. Lord knows she loved her aunt, but it was not merciful to scoff at the desires of a thirteen year old girl, even if you were fifty.

Not an actress but, there was only one thing she was certain she was not going to be and that was a veterinarian! Cold winters were bad enough, going out in the middle of freezing nights to tonic a colicky horse or patch up some farm kids' cat. Uh,uh. If they wanted to keep cats outside all night to tangle with every wild creature that came across its way, she would not be the one to go 'fix it!' And her fathers' work never did seem to end.

She reached the mailbox in front of her driveway and fumbled inside of it absently. Max must have gotten the mail, or else there wasn't any.

Her dad would probably still be sleeping off the effects of last night's calving. Early for spring calving. It was only January 20, in the old year of our lord, as Aunt Claudia would say. But he'd received the call at eleven o'clock last night and he still wasn't back when she left for school this morning.

Trudging up the drive she hesitated long enough to look for the old blue Ford pick up that usually stood in front of the car shed. It wasn't there. 'Robert McMurray to the everlasting rescue again!' She thought and kicked the rough stones in the driveway as she stomped off to the barn.

After she entered she stood staring at the white heads of the cows. She pulled a silly face at them and waited for her eyes to accustom themselves to the dimness inside.

The double doors opened behind her and she jumped. It was Max. He was sixty one years old but could have fooled a lot of people if they tried to guess. He looked much younger from working all of his life on the Double D; he could out tough if out against anyone she knew.

Max liked to point out that not many kids these days could keep up wid the ol' man. Max's 'kids' ranged in age from about fourteen to forty.

"Daddy didn't get much sleep, Max. You should have kept him in," she said to the farm hand. She knew that Max had been able to talk common sense to her father in the past; when he didn't pass on his extra work to the other vet in town, Carl Davies. Her tone of voice made it sound like he should have done it this time.

"Nope, and you won't either tonight if I don't give you a hand, he replied," as if he hadn't heard her accusation. "It's gonna' blow us out tonight. Weather man's predicting ten inches and, it's just about on us."

It looked like Aunt Claudia was right again. "Where did he have to go to, Max?" she asked, thumping the feeding switch. When it started to grind out the feed smoothly she grabbed a fork and settled into mucking out the stalls. From the looks of the floor the cows had been in all day. When Max didn't answer right away she stopped and leaned against the handle. Looking at him with a determined frown, she waited.

"Petersburg," he finally said, without stopping. "There's a bitch done up with pups and she ain't gettin' on with having 'um."

"Aww, Max, what did you have to let him go for?" she asked, pleadingly. "Couldn't you have talked him out of it?" Tossing the pitchfork aside she walked slowly over to the hay and sat down on one of the bales. Hunching her shoulders she put her chin in her hands.

It was her way keep from crying and Max knew it. He'd never seen her cry; even as a little kid. It didn't look like she was going to start now, either. He went back to work and dismissed it; allowing her to stew with her own thoughts for a couple of minutes. When the time drew on too long he gently prompted her by saying, "you're not getting anything done that way, missy."

Jessie took a deep breath and went back to work. The pet name didn't bother her at all. It was just Max's way of talking. He'd called her that since she was a baby.

Melissa had been her mother's name and Max had thought she looked enough like her to be a junior. Melissa died of pneumonia when Jessie was two. She didn't remember her but, wished she could.

The wind howling around the barn made them both look up. "Yeah, it's gonna blow us right out," Max said again, nodding. "Reccon we ought to get this work done on a quick. Claudia's got the chickens done; knowing how much you love them. She wanted to keep it a secret but, as I don't believe in them I figured I'd tell you.

"In your own good time," She said, sniffing. She picked up the pace of her own work as the wind began to moan loudly against the barn. It was a sound she'd always hated and they worked in silence as her nerves became taught.

"Spooks a commin' callin', "Max coaxed beginning an old game that seemed to soothe her nerves. "You know you gotta name um."

"That was Clark," she said, as a whine whipped around them. A high pitched whistle came in a few seconds, but it was over quite quickly.

"An' thar's Fast Freddy!" Max pronounced. A low roar followed and Max named it before she could think of one.

"Thar's Elviraaaaah," he droned out. "That one was too good to pas up. Next one's for you."

"Nuh, uh. I'm out of here. I'm fired," she sighed and added, "done."

"You're not gonna wait for an old man?" he asked, whining pathetically.

"Only if you quit putzing around and put a little muscle into it," she answered.

"Missy, I had none of those for fourty years and not much of them then," he said. "But, I can still pull my share even if you don't have the manners to help. Besides, you didn't beat me by much," he continued, as he went into the old tack room and hung up his shovel. "The bawdy old things will pig it up in no time. Can't pasture them on ice and mud but, with a good snow should be able to stick them out in the morning, though."

He was just rambling, Jessie new. The way he would talk to the men when he was younger and the Double D was the place to work. 'When I say the, I mean thee place to work,' Jessie thought wryly. Two thousand head of prime Herefords...back when her father was a youth and he went off to 'Vet' school.

Her father had an opportunity to inherit a ranch and save on the mending of what was his when he came home. But, Gramps had no foresight. Dealing with animals was a risky business.

Sometimes when you have too much of a good thing it would backfire on you. By the time Robert McMurray graduated it was too late for the cattle to benefit from his knowledge. They died of an unknown disease and there wasn't a veterinarian near enough to get to them and 'fix em' as Max would say. What had gone wrong was a mystery even to him.

The government men came and ordered them disposed of properly, and it cost Gramps savings to do it. The only thing spared was the Double D itself and her father sold most of the land off to set up his practice. The Ford wasn't back when she stepped out of the barn but that was only thing she could see. The snow was coming down all right. The house was about sixty feet from where she stood and you couldn't even see a shadow of it. Putting her head down against the onslaught she gripped the fence rail in her left hand and guessed her way back.

She could hear Max behind her and knew he was continuing to talk to her to get her home. It was the way they had gone many times before. Him always one step behind to make sure she didn't falter; him always the one to keep her safe.

They reached the outer door and were met by Aunt Claudia with two blankets. She'd gotten her part prepared. The fire was lit and there was hot chocolate on the hearth. The third blanket lay on the rug near enough to keep toasted and far enough away to avoid the sparks and the table was already set so that they could eat a hasty meal.

"Daddy call?" Jessie asked, as she slumped in a chair. "No but, Mike Thomas did. Your father will be home soon. He's bringing the dog with him," Claudia answered. Slipping a cup of coffee into Max's hand she sat in her own chair and watched out a window to a storm through which she couldn't see.

"That's a bitch, Claude," Max corrected as he sipped is chocolate and avoided her eyes by looking intently into the steam.

He was baiting Aunt Claudia and she knew it. She ignored him and went back to searching the storm.

"Dog can't have pups," he continued. He took another slow drink and leaned back into his seat with the air of an expert. "This one's gonna...""

"Oh, stop it you fool!" Claudia snapped. "In my day men wouldn't dare talk like that in front of a lady!"

"Who's a lady? You see a lady?" he asked Jessie, wide eyed, looking like he hadn't seen hide or hair of a lady in his life.
Jesse pointed in Aunt Claudia's direction, with a smirk on her face. "Nah, you're mistaken. That there's Claud!" he said with gusto.
Jessie nodded as though she were certain Aunt Claudia was indeed female.
"What...her, a girl? You could'a fooled me; with a name like that?"
That was enough for Jessie and she cracked up. No matter how many times they had been through this, and it wasn't enough to get stale, Aunt Claudia always fell for the bait.
"Maxwell Alamande Jefferson...The pride of Double D," Aunt Claudia scoffed, "never was a man could tell the difference between a Hereford and a lady. That's why he never married," she said to Jessie confidentially. "He always loved his work too much. Now if he'd done some time out of the barns and pastures he might know how to mind is manners but, as you can see..."
"The truck lights flashed past the window and Jessie leaped up to get the door. "Coat, Jessie," Aunt Claudia demanded.
"I've got it," Jessie said, snatching it from the rack "You want to get the lights on in the clinic, Max? He'll put her in the wagon, I'm sure."
"But, if he don't, holler and I'll come and help fetch her in. Don't you try," Max ordered.
They knew the routine well enough. Many times over the years Robert had brought home the troubles of neighboring farmers and pet owners. Usually enough to keep several crates and box stalls occupied.
The lights were more than that. The table that the animal would use needed to be fresh and a sterile area prepared, including surgical tools. Max, through practice, was the most efficient and went to work putting things in order. There was no hurry. He'd be done before Robert was ready for him.

Jessie propped the screen door with a brick kept for the purpose, and plowed her way towards the red tail lights of the truck. Her father was hauling a wooden sled from the back and nodded toward the front door of the Ford.

"Keep her company," he shouted over the storm. "I'm going to blanket her better before I take her out. She's a short hair."

"Max's in the shop," she said, over her shoulder. "He's ready to help you get her out if you need him."

Jessie opened the driver's side door and eased herself in. She could feel the shivers of the dog through the seat. "Big dog," she thought, "Max must have known." She slid the blanket off the dogs' head and began to soothe her with her voice and hands.

The dog was a Dalmatian, she noted. This was the first time she had ever seen one, except in her father's books. This was not a real useful dog in a farming community.

"I'll bet you don't like the winters and I'll also bet you don't know that you picked a rotten time to have your puppies." She crooned, "Now if you did you would have told your master to make sure you would have none except in summer."

The Dalmatian rolled her eyes as if to say, 'no kidding' and Jessie laughed.

The bitch whined at the sound and struggled to move. Jessie held onto her firmly, waiting for to her relax. For a moment it seemed as if she would settle down and then with a burst of energy she twisted in Jessie's grasp and used her nose to burrow into the blanket.

"I know girl," Jessie whispered. The Dalmatian grew more frantic and Jessie could see that it was senseless to fight her. She pulled the blanket aside and let her have her way.

It was dark in the truck and she felt secluded with the white snow hiding the outside world. Not knowing how long it would be before her father got there with the sled, she would not take the chance that he might just open the door while the Dalmatian and her first puppy were uncovered.

With the puppy having just been born he was still very wet and the danger of chill was apparent. Whether she would bite to protect her new pup or allow her to be near it, Jessie did not know but, she would have to take the chance. She reached hesitantly across the young mother and locked the door; so that no one could open it until she had asked her dad what he wanted her to do.

With the other various breeds of dogs there had been no problem in winter births although they were few. But, this was the first time that she'd ever been in such a difficult position.

It didn't take long for the mother to clean her pup and she was resting before there was a harsh rap on the side of the truck. They'd found their way back and we're feeling the way along the side.

Jessie reached along side of her self and cranked the window down. She had pulled the blanket over her charges and she shifted herself back over to her side of the truck catching her breath as the wind rushed at her.

The handle on the other side clacked and she knew they were near enough to hear before she pushed herself partly out of the window and called for them. "Daddy she's had one!" she hollered, "what should I do with it?"

"Wait," her father replied.

Sliding back down in the seat she rolled up the window and did as she was told. Jessie could feel the motion of the Dalmatian as she began to shudder once again.

Great, she thought. Now that the work of having the first pup was done This dog had time to lay back and freeze to death right before her eyes.

"Hey, you," she said, evenly, "you are not going to get away that easy. You have a long way to go. Don't give up on us now."

"Jessie?" her father called.

"Yes?" she answered, nervously.

"Will she let you take the pup?"

"I don't know."

"Put your hand on her head and talk to her. If she's quiet I want you to reach in a way that she can see and take the puppy. Don't let her see you! If she growls get out of there in a hurry. Quick! Do you hear me? If she growls at all...you get out!" he instructed her.

"Right," Jessie answered. Her right hand had been on the Dalmatian the whole time and Jessie wasn't afraid of her, but she was calm and cautious as she felt underneath the blanket for the newly born puppy. Once she had it in her hand she watched the face of mother for the curl of lips that would come from and over protective dam. There was none and she had the pup in her lap before she knew it. This was one time she was grateful for the dark.

"I've got it," she called.

"Put it in your coat front. You can bring it in. I'll get the other door. Stay away from the dog. She might smell him on you," her father directed.

Jessie opened the door when she had the puppy stored safely in her coat and it was buttoned snugly around it. She didn't stop to watch the process of fetching the mother, but headed directly for the kitchen door. Though her father had parked the truck as near to the door as possible; Jessie had difficult time breathing into the wind; and was gasping when she reached it. This was the fiercest storm she could remember. Aunt Claudia opened the door for her and she hurried inside.

"She had one. It's here," Jessie said, popping the buttons of her coat loose. She handed the puppy to her aunt and headed back into the night.

They had the mother strapped on the sled, she noted. It was no wonder as the ground was already thick with snow. She would travel easier that way.

Taking hold of the side she plowed alongside until they were in the house and right into the clinic section. They worked quickly from there and no one spoke until they had the dog settled and she was ready for what ever might have to be done to deliver her of the rest of her burden.

"Go take a break," Robert MacMurray said to his daughter. "It's going to be hours before we're done here."

Jessie turned on or heel. She wouldn't be allowed to stay in the room with them and she knew it, but he didn't have to come up with excuses. It was bad, she knew and he always made her stay out of way when there were complications. He would tell her all about it later, after she lay in bed, wide awake; wondering if he was using a sharp scalpel to do a caesarean section. If the dog was lying in pain as he helped her deliver one after another. If she was dying or if his surgery was a success; she wouldn't know until it after it was over.

She stepped in the living room that was alongside the clinic and wrapped herself up in a blanket to warm up before her Aunt decided it was time to send her upstairs to bed. The house was huge, but she had the unfortunate position of having her room directly over the same room were those same puppies would be born. She wouldn't be able to hear what was going on beneath her but she would wonder. She wouldn't sleep up there tonight.

An overstuffed cream colored recliner sat perched before the large ranch style hearth; with a blazing fire snapping comfortably inside of it. Jessie curled up in the chair and gazed into the flames.

This was the family room and it was her favorite. The Double D was still a showpiece. There was nothing over this room but the vaulted ceilings. An entire wall of windows arose from the floor to the top on the sunny side of the room;

the other side a wall of books. Near them was an enormous walnut desk and its richness was brought out by the heavy paneling that covered the rest of the walls; making the room smell like being in a dense forest. The furnishings were lush and comfortable. It wasn't long before the crackling of the fire had lulled Jessie to sleep.

2
Seven to Choose From

She was sleeping soundly when Aunt Claudia finally roused her from the chair. The room was light and when she looked out of the window she had to squint from the glare of the sun and new fallen snow.

"What time is it?" she groaned.

"Six thirty. I thought you went to bed. They just finished up. The dog had ten but, she lost two," Aunt Claudia said matter-of-factly.

Jessie knew the odds well enough. It was good that they had managed to keep that many alive.

Her father was sitting in a chair beside the large pen watching his patients, but he got up we saw Jessie come in.

"You're up early. There's no school, if you had not heard," he said, easily.

"I haven't gone to bed, if you didn't notice," she laughed, gesturing at her rumpled clothes, "and I thought that I wouldn't be able to sleep. You need some."

"I see," he said and nodded. "The pups are white. Do you suppose their misfits?" she asked, crouching down beside the gate.

They were in a large wooden box inside of a pen that was made of chain link. It was about four feet wide and six feet long running along one wall of the room.

There were three of these cages. Her father believed the animals kept in them should have the room. The house was certainly big enough to accommodate them.

In the next room over there were stalls for large animals; and in a cubicle between them he kept his tools. Off again toward the front of the house was his office and waiting room, for those who brought their animals instead of having him go to them.

Jessie wondered why the one who owned this dog had not brought her in, instead of making her father chase out in this weather and back. It wasn't good for the dog and it didn't help her dad when he'd been up so much the night before.

'There are a lot of inconsiderate people,' she thought. 'It seems that they are even worse when it came to their vet. They make a big show of loving their pets, but when it comes to their health the truth about how they feel comes through.'

"Where's the owner?" Jessie asked. "Will he be stopping out to see his dogs?"

"If he can get through," he sighed. "The weather stops more than school, you know."

"Why didn't he bring her in?" Jessie demanded. It was unfair to ask him, she knew but, it didn't stop her. She resented the owner of this dog bitterly even though she had not met him."

"Jessie, it's my duty, as you well know. I'm the only vet in these parts. If the client calls, I go. I have to and we've been through this before. I mind!" he said, exasperated by her question. "I know this dog. I knew it was her time. If I could have foreseen her going into labor early I would have brought her here a week ago but, I didn't! If he'd called and I could not have gone I would have worried myself sick that he had brought her in to Carl Davies in Three corners and maybe died on the way. That's twenty miles farther away…I'm a Vet, Jessie. It's my job to be there. I sure wish you could understand that. I have no idea why you can't get close to an animal, but I'm sorry. I'm sorry for you. You'll never know the love and loyalty that comes from a good dog," he said, retreating into his lab.

Jessie knew that part of the reason her father was so upset was because he was tired and she shouldn't be angry with him or say the thing she was going to say but she said it anyway.

"Yeah, well maybe in order to care about them I would have to see you take care of yourself first!"

"I will," he chuckled "Tomorrow."

"I don't see what's so funny," she said turning away from the kennel.

"You'll harp at me for week over this and you're the one who slept on the couch last night," he replied smugly.

"At least I slept," she grumbled. "There's no hope for you. You aren't going to listen to me anyway. If someone called you right now you'd go."

He straightened up, and strode across a room until he stood less than a foot in front of her. He studied her face for a moment and then scowled.

"I've raised you on this farm since you were little girl; hoping that someday you would learn to appreciate it. I would have done it no different, Jessie, even if I had known that you would hate it. Because, somehow, I know that if you had been raised in a house with servants and precious antiques, you have still found a reason to hate it," he accused. "No matter where you go, young lady, you'll still have to deal with the fact that in this world, even if you're rich, you still have to work. This is my job…it's what I do. It's what we live on, and Jessie, I like what I do," he said, gently.

Her eyes glossed with tears, and she turned away, just as the phone rang. He went to pick it up in his office.

The noise woke the puppies and she went over to watch them. Her father hadn't told her if they were what he called misfits. The name he used for any animal that was born not looking the way it should, or the way it was expected; like a dark horse delivering a white colt. It happened. She knew the basics of genetics from things that her father had told her when he was explaining the 'what happened to create this animal' things to her. All of the information that could be passed down from the parents that made it possible to determine what might come from a breeding. If he bred a bay horse that had AABB type to a bay horse that had AABB type you would have a bay foal that was AABB. It was kind of a reddish color. Nothing else was possible. But, that was the simplest definition that her father had ever given her; and she still didn't know what that AABB stood for.

She supposed she should show more interest. It might make him happier. If he was still determined a stay in this awful town it wouldn't pay to make it worse for him by giving him something more worry about. They didn't talk about it that often, after all. Sometimes she felt she would burst if she kept her feelings inside.

This was usually how it happened, and just like now she felt guilty about how she behaved. He'd spent a lot of years in college to be a veterinary surgeon. He'd never give it up; not this place or this town; and she should be happy for him.

Jessie wasn't paying much attention to the squirming babies; only really staring blankly at them but, her attention was caught when a very small one squealed in pain. Somehow he'd managed to get part way out from under his litter mates and was presently fighting his way toward his mother's teat.

With paws waving frantically he beat his way out from between them and rolled down and away from the breakfast he had fought so hard for.

The humps of the other puppies bodies were a huge obstacle in front of his blind face but, pushing himself forward with its hind legs he somehow managed to get back on top.

Jessie sighed, not realizing she'd been holding her breath, when a shift in the mass sent the pup tumbling right back to the bottom of the pile. A second later she had the gait opened and was inside with them. She didn't watch the mother's face as she picked up the runt, lifting him toward a now empty teat.

At first he wouldn't take it; even when she held his nose against it. The feel of hands against his body made him struggle; as within the confines of its mother's womb. With the tip of her pinky, Jessie opened his mouth and adjusted his head so that the teat was inside. When she took her finger away the teat was in his mouth. His tongue pushed at it for a second and she was afraid he'd spit it out; but finally, he realized what he had and began sucking. She continued to hold him, afraid that any sudden change in position would distract him.

Robert MacMurray made a noise behind her and after she looked his way; he continued into the room.

"I didn't want to startle you," he said quietly. "That was Mike Thomas on the phone. He owns them pups that you're fondling. He said that he'd be over in about two hours; the plows are clearing up his road now."

"Is he disappointed about the two that were lost?" she asked, releasing the runt and getting to her feet. She spared a kind pat to the mother who had spent her time happily cleaning her pups as Jessie had sat beside her.

"No. Smaller litters are usually stronger for it," he replied.

"That's not what you would usually say," she remarked, leaving the kennel "You said if the dam has the milk that they usually do fine."

"Usually," he agreed "if the dog is sturdy enough. Lady Gwen isn't a big dog for her kind, though. She'll probably lose a lot of weight with the ones she has now. It would have been better if she had been older. I have a diet made up for her but, that's a lot of milk to produce."

"You're worried," Jessie said, surprised. The mother looked okay to her. She glanced back at her again anyway. She looked the same; to all appearances; a good healthy dog.

"Why?" she asked.

"Because she's small for her kind," he answered. "They have it the toughest. The runts...Just like the one you were holding a minute ago. He'll be lucky if he makes it.

"No, your wrong," she insisted. "He would have made it. I just wanted to be in by him. You should have seen him fight!"

Her father shook his head and said, "Jessie, I know why you were in There. I did the same when he was born. He was the last one and Gwen was very tired. It took a long time for him to be born. That's a lot of stress on a small puppy.

"Gwen?"

"Lady Gwenevere of Camelot," he answered, gesturing toward the kennel. "That's a lot of dog. You might add the champion when you wish."

"Whew!" Jessie whistled. "Are the puppies all right? I mean...well, they're white."

"They're fine. They won't get their spots for a while yet, so it's hard to know what they'll look like in the end, but they're perfectly healthy. A Dalmatian earns his spots." He chuckled. "Except for the runt; he's formed the best of all of them, so much as I can tell at this stage, but as I said, he's had a hard time."

"He would have made it without me," Jessie said trying to ease is fears.

"We'll see. In the meantime you ought to get out and see if Max needs you."

"I should have gone to bed," she groaned but, she was already on her way to the door.

Max must have been up at five. Jessie had just eaten a small breakfast and hurried out to help with the chores but, the cows were already milked and out to pasture. He'd plowed much of the snow aside for them but, some were still standing knee deep in places where the drifts blocked their path from the outer shelter.

She could hear the plow working its way up the drive and waited for it.

"There's half the stalls in there for you," Max shouted above the noise of the tractor. "Get some straw down and cover them. We don't need hoof rot from the wet."

Jessie nodded and headed away. Her work had begun.

3
Kill the Runt

Mike Thomas had arrived by the time Jessie was finished. She could hear her father talking with him as she walked by the office. It was Robert McMurray's policy that no one from the house went in when a client was there unless invited; and she waited, instead, in the hall.

It was the first time she had ever witnessed her father go completely against himself. The hairs on the back of her neck prickled as she listened.

"I'll put the runt down in a couple of days," her father was saying, "when she won't be distressed so badly. I'm sure it will last that long."

"I don't want it making any demands on her." 'That must have been the owner.' Jessie thought. She clenched her teeth and nearly growled herself. He was inconsiderate and cruel!

"It's too small to do much of that. As I said, it would do no good to distress her in the condition that she's in now," her father said.

She could hear them coming to the door and decided it was best if she made herself scarce. Turning on her heel she marched into the kitchen and slumped into the nearest chair.

"Problems?" Aunt Claudia asked, lightly.

"Of a sorts," Jessie said, testily. "Have you ever known daddy to kill a perfectly healthy animal just because it is a little bit too small?"

"There must be other reasons, Jessie," Aunt Claudia answered. "If it has to suffer and then die anyway..."

"He said so himself..." Jessie choked. Taking a deep breath she went on. She was in control but, she was bristling. "He said it was the best formed of them. Why does he have to kill it? I've seen him nurse tiny babies before...he won't even give this one a chance!"

"Are you willing to?" Aunt Claudia asked, gently. "Can you spare the time it will take and have the patience to tend it every two hours until it can take care of itself?"

"I have school!" Jessie said. The tone of her voice emphasized the unfairness of it.

"Would you if you didn't have school?" Aunt Claudia asked, evenly.

"Of course I would. You can't just give up like that. It's criminal!" Jessie snapped.

"And while you father is giving all his attention to your runt, do you suppose he should neglect his other work? You're not the only one whose time is taken up," Aunt Claudia answered placing the bread dough she had just made into a loaf pan so it could rise.

She watched the changing expression on her nieces face and knew Jessie needed time to come to the understanding that not all was fair in the ways of nature. It wasn't fair that some animals couldn't make a go of it. Those were the facts.

She had felt sorry for Jessie each time that hardship of veterinary practice had made itself felt; the animals that were beyond hope. It was the reason, though her brother couldn't see it; that Jessie was afraid to become attached to animals; even the horse that Jessie had once asked him for.

Robert would have gotten one for her a long time ago if Claudia hadn't intervened. She had told him that Jessie wouldn't care for it but, that wasn't true. Jessie would have cared for it too much and too many things can happen to a horse. Well, here it was now. If she kept her mouth shut this time that pup was as good as going to break Jessie's heart. Maybe it would be better to have that, than give her false hopes. Claudia kept silent.

Max came shuffling in and headed directly for the coffeepot. He nodded at Jessie and poured himself a cup. Jessie tried to smile at him and failed miserably.

"What's up, pup?" he chuckled. It was one of his expressions albeit badly timed

Jessie winced and got up abruptly. "I'm going to my room" she said evenly. "I've had enough of pups for today."

4

Stormy Knight's Colt

Robert closed the door after his client left and stood with his hand on the knob as if he would open it again and call Mike back. He didn't like to be deceptive. When he heard the car pull away he strode deliberately from the clinic; not looking in the direction of the kennel.

Claudia winced as he entered the kitchen. She could tell that her brother was in the same kind of pain as Jessie

"Coffee?" she asked him.

"Black," he answered, taking a chair and watching her pour it. "You might say we have seven pups, Claudia. Mike decided to have the runt put down."

"I've heard," Claudia mumbled. "It seems that your daughter over heard you talking with him."

"She's taken a liking to that runt," he nodded bleakly, taking the cup and thanking her. "Why do you suppose, the first time I can get her interested in something living I have to take it away?"

Claudia sat opposite from him and didn't answer.

"I called Bryan Corren this morning. He'd asked me to check around for a buyer for one of his horses. I think I'll take it for Jessie."

"Why?" Claudia asked coldly. She was startled by his quick change of subject and angered by his solution. "Do you think you can make it up to her, or do you think it would be better to teach her to replace something when she loses it, as if it were material? It's not an old coat we're talking about here and Jessie certainly is old enough to know the difference!"

"I'm not doing it, Claudia. I'm not putting that pup down." Claudia eyes widened and she sat there mute. "There's nothing wrong with it and if he gets a few days nourishment from his dam I'm pretty sure I can raise him myself. The mother is so weak though. I can barely get her to eat."

"We'll all help" Claudia offered "and Jessie already…"

"Jessie is not to know," he interrupted. "If we fail, well, it wouldn't do to have her hopes brought up just to have to…" He breathed in sharply and wrung his hands in appeal.

"Okay" Claudia said. "She won't know. When he's old enough, you tell me and we'll put him up in my room."

"Thanks," he sighed.

"Maybe a horse would take him off her mind?" she offered.

"That's what I'm hoping for now; I'm buying a horse and stealing a dog," he sighed, getting wearily from the table, "and it'll probably be the last thing I do in the veterinary field."

The door closed behind him and in a minute Claudia could hear the big Ford pull away. He didn't have any appointments. She knew where he was going, and it amazed her that he would go so far is spare his daughter's heart. What he needed was some sleep.

Some of the roads were still thick with snow and he had to plow slowly through them, but in time soon enough he was at the gate of Bryan Corran's farm. It stood open waiting for him to enter but, he paused. He almost turned back and made the three mile trip back to the Double D. What he was doing was wrong and he knew it. It had caused him to hesitate more than once today and he didn't like the feeling of uncertainty he was having.

He knew he was going against the way he and Melissa had agreed to raise her but, some part of him said that this was his only chance to keep Jessie interested in animals and a large part of him wanted her to feel the connection with animals that he felt. This was the easy way out and he knew it.

He put the truck and gear and slowly pulled into the drive; to the sound of the snow crunching under the tires; grinding and squeaking as if in protest.

Bryan was coming from the house to meet him and he didn't linger in the truck to think any longer on the rights and wrongs of the matter. His mind was made up for better or worse.

"Hi, Doc," Bryan chirped. "Have I got a horse for you! He's prime stock; the best of the best." Clapping Robert on the back he indicated the way into the stables.

"I've seen all your best, Bryan," Robert laughed. "You don't have to sell me."

"Not this one you haven't; I only acquired him two months ago. Another vet looked him over on account of it was over 200 miles north of here; so you ain't seen him yet."

"Now, if you just bought him, then why are you selling?" Robert asked. "It seems to me you would keep him until the summer to see how he does and get a better price."

"Normally I would do just that," Bryan laughed. "But, it was for the profit you see. The man's barn burned down and he had to sell his excess quick. I got him for a song and five others like him. Now I need the room! So, I just as soon see how the others do and part with this one. There he is," Bryan offered, pointing to a narrow stall. "You look him over yourself and see what he's worth."

A light gray head chinned itself over the manger and the distinctive features a finely crafted Arabian looked back at him.

"Whew!" Robert whistled. "Is the rest of him like that?" He didn't wait for Bryan to answer and instead slipped a lead rope on the colts' halter, opened the gate and led him out of the stall. The gelding's body was a bit heavy from winter hay but, from the beginning Robert could see the horse had merit.

"Your daughter could show him. He's that good," Bryan said easily "I'll walk him out for you. Just you watch the way he moves. He's as light and graceful as a cat and as gentle as a kitten."

Robert scrutinized each movement, looking for defect. There was none apparent enough to harm his already good opinion of the colt.

Moving up along side the grey he began his examination; his hands sliding across the shoulder; down the chest the legs and the barrel; covering each part of the horse in a sure and even pattern.

He nodded and reached in his bag for a stethoscope and using it; he heard the beating of the great heart and clear breathing of this almost too good to be true horse.

He began taking even more care, looking for fault. He studied the eyes and ears as if wanting to find something wrong. Some reason to turn this horse down.

"Is he registered?" he heard himself ask; as though it was required for Jessie to own a horse with a pedigree. There was no need for one with a gelding that could not produce offspring.

"He is," Bryan answered, "with terrific lineage; classical Arabians; with many a champion among them. I have a stallion in the loose stall that is really no better than the colt you're looking at. As a matter of fact it's his sire, Stormy Knight. "You can look him over as much as you want. It seems to me you were never so thorough when I called you to go over horse I wanted to buy!" he muttered.

Robert stopped his inspection and stood staring at the gray withers in front of him. He couldn't even fault the grey colt for his size. Even at Jessie's maturity; she would not outgrow him; and he was sure that this horse was not too much for her to handle.

"It's not the horse. The guess I was hoping I would have an excuse not to buy him. Or, maybe, the reason is more that I don't know if what I'm doing is wrong. It doesn't matter, Bryan, your price is actually low. I'll by him," Robert said, firmly.

"Why wrong?" Bryan asked. "She's a young girl Robert. You can't expect her to just take things in stride. There'll be enough time for that when she gets older. Don't expect that this is just going to make her forget the puppy. You're just taking away part of the sting; that's all. I think having something to love, like a good horse, would be just the ticket for helping her have good feelings again. Lucky girl; at least she has a father that can provide her with that."

Robert frowned and reflected that in future he might not be able to do that. It all hinged on whether Mike Thomas would press charges against him if the pup lived and he found out that his vet went against his wishes.

Bryan had raised three daughters of his own and Robert took his advice more easily because of it. He was glad that he had told Bryan the problem. He had just left out the part about the puppy not being destroyed.

"I hope you're right. Could you deliver him?" he asked. "I have rounds."

"Is tomorrow morning soon enough?" the farmer asked happily. Robert nodded and began to turn away. "In future I will be sure to vet your horses more thoroughly," he said turning back "and thank you for making this a little easier Bryan. I hope you're right about that sting."

"Good enough, doc.; in the morning then," Bryan said, smiling. The farmer watched him as he made his way back to the truck. Only when it was lost down the road did he lead the colt back to his stall.

5
Dream Come True

essie ate her breakfast in silence as she had her supper the night before, even taking her self to bed early; without so much as saying good night. The only thing she had done the night before; was to spend time watching the little runt in his kennel. For this while, at least, he was safe.

She rode in the truck to school. Her father was making his morning rounds and she often rode with him but, this morning they were not chatting as they usually did and Robert offered nothing to cheer her up. As soon as he stopped in front of the school she slipped out and shut the door with a sort of finality.

Margie Lewis spotted her and waved her over where she was standing against the building. Several of her friends were there and she knew they'd be hurt if she had seen them and didn't go to them. Picking her chin up, she walked over to them; the smile on her face belying her pain.

Anita Whitman was talking to Adam Berglund; otherwise known as the greatest looking guy in class. Jessie noted the way Anita had her arm against his and made purposely to the other side of the group from them.

"Hey, Jessie," Margie began "how'd you like the vacation?"

"They'll just tack it on at the end of the year;" Paul Zelmer answered for her. "In spring when it's most convenient."

"Paul's fishing is going to suffer, poor boy," Anita Whitman laughed.

"Who likes to fish any way?" Margie asked, making a face of disgust. "You ever watch them clean fish?"

"Well your family eats them every Friday night," Paul laughed. "How do you think those little filets start out?"

"In a store, silly," she answered, sweetly. Jessie smiled but didn't fall into their conversation and she privately thanked Paul for unwittingly saving her. It seemed forever before the bell rang and when it did she buried herself in her work.

On a normal day Claudia was well into her second TV program before noon. She did get a glimpse of them occasionally today; in between visits to eight little white pups.

She told Robert that she would check on them thru the day; even though he knew that she would. Checking meant every few hours or so but she'd spent more time in with them than out. 'Thinking, planning, scheming,' her brother would call it. He didn't have any idea the solution that she'd come up with. He wouldn't like it if he did.

It meant keeping the pup alive. Making him catch up a little faster than the others and that meant food and warmth; whenever he wanted it; for as long as she could before the owner came back.

At one thirty she was still holding him against his mother when she heard the van pull in. She had given Gwen food out of her hand as she sat with her; and neither she or her pup really needed her right now. Still, she didn't want to leave them.

"Okay, pup. I have to go," she said, getting to her feet. It was getting harder for her to do and she realized she would be plenty stiff tonight from sitting on the floor for so long.

Slipping on her coat she went out to meet Jessie's new horse.

The pup stayed on Jessie's mind no matter how hard she tried and the day dragged by so slowly that it surprised her when it finally did end.

She left the school, without meeting her friends outside as she usually did. No matter how long the puppy was going to be there she wanted to share it with him.

Lancelot and Lady Gwenevere. It was a mistake and she knew it. The worst thing she had done was to name him. It was one more thing to make him special to her. As if he where hers to name.

'Other people's pets; it was always someone else's. Her dad ought to have a sign on his door; 'you break 'em — we fix 'em' like a service station that deals in living things,' she thought.

It wasn't all of the work her father did as a veterinarian. She realized that. Actually, most of the time; it was just regular maintenance, like getting shots and worming. But when they came in sick and dying because the owners didn't know how to take care of what they had...then, well it just seemed wrong.

You hated knowing that you were sending them back into the same situation; even when the owners didn't seem to realize that what they were doing caused harm. You would tell them; they would say that they understood but, in a month or so they were back. And if it continued...then you had to get in touch with the authorities and go thru the process of taking the animals away.

That happened once. It was a horse stable. The owners rented out the horses to touring city folk. City people want to ride the horsies but, they don't really know how and none of them seemed to notice that the stables were so awful. They just must have thought that, well...horsies make messes. That's why they don't keep them in the city, right?

So, no one said anything about the poor horses or the owner. The horses just got sicker. Before the investigator was called some of them had even died.

They had all fought hard to keep the rest of them alive and with perseverance, all nine of them did. All of them were placed at nice farms once they were well enough but, that they had gone thru so much to get there!

Joey Douglas owned two of them. A pinto pony he had named Prince and a large sorrel gelding that was already named King by the people who had owned them before.

He rode over to her farm a couple times a week and Adam Berglund joined him; most of the time on King. He lived right next door to Joey and just down the road from her. They were the best of friends.

It had a little to do with the way she felt about Adam that she wanted a horse of her own. They had a great time riding double and talking but, it would be a lot easier if she could ride alongside.

She was almost home before it occurred to her that they might be by. The horses had to have been kept in with the storm and would need exercise. If the boys found out about the litter they might help her convince Mike Thomas to let Lancelot live.

Jessie stopped in her tracks, gaping in disbelief at the pasture. Her luck couldn't be so bad! The grey horse gazing back at her meant her father had one more reason to say no.

If the horse wasn't too sick he'd be in his own stable. Now she'd have to help her father with him and Lance would be forgotten.

Tears welled in her eyes as she began walking toward the ruin of her plan. And he just stood there!

"What did you do, horse?" she choked as she neared him. "Did you get into the oats or did you swallow a wire?"

He was about twenty feet away from the rail and she leaned on it to keep her balance. The snow was very deep along the fence.

The grey horse just kept looking at her. Not moving to greet her but, looking so much like he wanted to that she had to forgive him. Oh, it was hard. She had to remind herself that he knew nothing about the trouble he was causing.

"Come on," she sniffed. "You don't have to be afraid of me. I'm not here to ride you or to vet you or make you do anything you don't want. Just let me see you."

Nickering lightly he took a step forward. When he stopped again she ducked between the rails and stood inside with him. A dumb thing to do when you haven't been told anything about a large animal but, it wasn't the first chance she had ever taken. 'Yet, maybe it would be best if I wasn't in here with a strange horse while my thoughts are still on Lance,' She thought suddenly.

Before she could turn and retrace her steps the gelding began walking towards her at an even and direct pace. Jessie froze. About the worst thing she could do now, would be to turn her back on him, and the second would be to show fear.

"Hey, boy, come on," she said to him. He was only about a foot away when he stopped and she could have reached out to touch him if she had wanted to. Her hand had nothing in it for a treat but, she held it out as if it did.

"That's the way. I hope you don't mind sharing this here pasture. I'm not going anywhere until you decide to let me, okay?" she promised.

The rail was against her back and she felt trapped. He towered over her. How he managed to look so small out in the snow she didn't know but, standing in front of her now he was like a giant grey ghost; almost not real.

His head swiveled and he whinnied before racing away to the other side of the pasture.

Joey and Adam's horses were sending up plumes of snow clouds as they cantered in the soft drifts along the shoulder of the road.

Jessie fell thru the bars of the fence as she pitched her self between them. She was trying to scramble to her feet in time not to be seen by her friends. They didn't need to see her fear any more than that grey monster did.

Picking herself up; she began hastily dusting off the clots of snow from her pants and seat in desperate flailing of her hands; it wasn't working. She looked frosted and no matter if they had seen her or not, they wouldn't miss this chance at a good laugh.

Groaning, she stood up straight and waited for them. Her father's guest was whinnying excitedly at the new arrivals. Prince and King were responding in heartfelt blasts of their own.

Jessie was hoping to watch them struggle to control their mounts but, her grin died on her face as she watched them reaching over the fence to stroke the neck of the grey horse. They had dismounted and were leading their horses along the fence.

The back door opened and she stared at her father as if he were an alien. He looked way too happy and Robert MacMurray never looked happy if there was something to worry about.

"Jessie," he said as if he were just acknowledging her presence. He stood next to her and they watched together as the boys brought in the colt.

Joey tied his pinto at the hitch and his smile of satisfaction gave him away as a conspirator.

"Do you have an appointment with them?" Jessie asked, looking confused. "They're acting as if they have a purpose."

"I think they're getting your horse ready," Robert responded. "I think it's about time you rode your own, don't you?"

"Mine?"

"I bought him last night and asked your friends if they would help me surprise you. He's as gentle as a kitten for his age," Robert said, smiling at the shroud of fresh snow covering her shoulders. "You could have waited with him."

"You saw!" she squeaked.

"Who didn't," he laughed. "That was some first introduction. It doesn't matter much, Jessie. Let's go collect your horse or do you expect the boys to do all the work?"

It was at that moment that Jessie realized why he had bought the colt. He had already destroyed Lancelot. Her heart pounding she whirled towards the house. She slipped a couple of times as she ran and didn't care. If he were gone she would never forgive her father, she vowed.

Throwing the door wide she skidded thru the kitchen and down the hall towards the clinic. Outside the door she stopped and panted trying to compose herself enough to keep the mother of the pups calm. As she entered the clinic she heard the back door click shut and the sound of her fathers heavy tread behind her.

Hurriedly she reached the kennel and sat down inside of it. Without taking the time to count she spied Lancelot and as relief flooded thru her she proceeded to count anyway; just to prove to herself that her own eyes weren't lying.

No one could have told her that she wouldn't be able to pick Lancelot out from among look a-like pups. She knew him instantly; and the spot verified what she already knew. Lancelot's luck charm; he had already earned a spot. Just one; on the inside of his right ear; and she had told herself that you couldn't be born lucky and not live.

"He's still there, Jessie," Robert asserted. He was surprised with how quickly she had found her pup amongst the litter and that he already thought of him as her pup. "I want him to be alright too but, you have to know…he might not get that chance. His life is not in your hands any more than it is mine."

"You bought him…the horse…to make me forgive you if Lance dies," Jessie accused. "We'll, it won't work and you can't just….just expect me to forget!"

"Maybe I did. It makes things easier when you can give your feelings to another animal when the one you want is the one you can't have. No matter how you feel that pup is not yours. His owner is Mike Thomas and this entire litter belongs to him."

"Why don't you buy him, then," she cried. "Tell him that I want this one. Oh, daddy I want him more than the horse!"

"It's not that simple and you know it," he sighed. "Gwen has to care for the others and she can't do that if the demands on her are too much for her to bear. Those pups are going to grow quickly. Now don't get your hopes up but, if I didn't think there was a chance for him he would already be gone."

Jessie stroked Lady Gwen. There were no growls in the cage; Gwen barely raised her head and Jessie could see for herself how weak the Dalmatian was; laying there with all those young ones nursing on her. Her hopes fell to making this young mother well enough to care for her young.

Now she knew the position her father had been placed in. It was his fault no more than it ever could have been placed on Gwen. If this dog's owner cared for her at all then she couldn't even blame him for wanting to put Lance down.

"She needs her rest, Jessie," Robert said quietly.

"I know…," she answered. She rose to her feet and left the kennel, closing the gate behind her. "I think I will go for a ride."

It was from her own guilt at blaming him; and almost allowing herself to hate him; for something that wasn't his fault. But, right now she felt she needed a ride. If for no other reason; than to have this time to sort out how to deal with the possibility; that her own father might 'have to' put Lance to sleep.

6
Whose Horse?

Joey and Adam had just finished saddling the grey colt when she came out of the house. They were expecting her to ride with them no matter what she had to say about it. Given enough time they would probably have come in after her. They'd done it before.

'These guys have a selfish streak in them and don't take no for an answer,' she thought. But, something about that had always been good for her. It had kept them friends when at times she would have rather fought.

"Ready to go," Joey asked pleasantly, "or do I get a try at the new horse?"

Jessie stopped and cocked her head at him, smiling impishly. "You sure he's not too much for you, pony boy? He's an Arabian and they have a pretty big reputation for being high strung."

"Might I?" he asked, stepping over to the side of the colt.

Some part of the fear she had felt in the pasture remained inside of her; even though the colt was nuzzling Adam with his ears tipped forward and his eyes showed no malice; she couldn't seem to shake it away. Not trying to appear eager she hesitated before making her decision.

"For you, and only you," she laughed. "Show me what you can do with a grown up horse, Joey."

Without a second to spare after her last word; she had snagged Prince's reigns and swung onto his back; turning him away from the grey Arabian she didn't give Joey a chance to change his mind.

"Hey Jessie, you wait up!" Adam called climbing aboard the restive King.

He was waiting for Joey to mount the new horse and was very unsure of leaving him alone. Even if Mr. McMurray did trust the colt he wasn't sure he would. Joey was stroking the grey neck of the colt and Adam hoped he would chicken out when it came to getting on him.

He would've offered to take him first if Joey hadn't been so cocky about having the first ride.

Jessie was afraid of her new horse; of that Adam was sure. He'd watched her escape from the pasture and had decided then that he would be with her until she was safe with the animal. Joey was barely able to ride King and only when Adam was there. He was awkward with large horses. Not really afraid of them as much as he was of the height from which he was perched. In the fields or in the stalls he was great, but not on a tall horse even if he did own them.

Holding King back, he shifted from keeping an eye on Jessie's retreating back and staying in a position where he could help Joey if trouble broke out with the colt. Horses were something of a specialty with him.

Joey dragged himself aboard the colt; his death grip on the saddle and the set of his bared teeth showing plainly how much he regretted being so out spoken.

When the colt shifted his weight to compensate for Joey's slow progress he nearly dropped back to the ground. Adams quick action stopped that humiliation. He grabbed the head stall of the colts' bridal and held it fast.

Nudging his knee over the back of the saddle Joey sat up and took over.

"If Jesse wants to give you Prince back and get on her own horse she'll have to wait for us, hey?" Adam grinned. "I ain't chasing her."

"Thanks," Joy said in answer. "Big horse."

"You'll get used to him. Somebody's going to have to if he's to get exercise. It doesn't seem as if Jesse's going to be the one to do it."

Joey looked at the horse between his knees and it dawned on him that Adam was probably right. Though Jesse didn't mind the height of King as he did, there was something really wrong about her and this colt.

Tightening his grip on the reigns Joey nudged the colt forward.

7
Mismatched

After five minutes of riding they finely caught up with Jesse. She was cantering the pony up a long flat hill. After that hill there was a grove of trees and she reigned in before entering; keeping her back to them in an 'I don't want to talk about it' attitude; she let the ponies head down the graze.

"Ready?" Adam asked, nodding at the hill. It was the only way to get up to Jessie; and on the other horses they would have comfortably raced up the hill in a canter. It wasn't steep and the horses seemed to love the game.

King backed playfully and pranced in eagerness. He wanted his head but Adam kept him in check. Joey would have had to ride up the hill first because Adam wanted to be back on Joey's heels if he lost control of the new horse. The gray stood motionless; his head thrown high; whinnying sharply at the pony at the top of the incline.

Pinching his knees against the colt's sides Joey braced for the inevitable. The grey charged; his stride lengthening. The hill came up too fast for him and he gathered himself sharply. Joey was losing ground in the saddle and snugged his fingers in the colt's thin mane hoping it would help him hold on.

The slant of the saddle as he ascended the hill was just enough. Each time the colt lunged forward he found himself just a little lower on the beast's back. The stirrups fell off of his boots and for a terrifying second he could envision the frozen ground coming up to meet him; and then he was still. The colt stopped at the top of the hill of his own accord.

Joey pushed him self away from the colt and landed, mercifully on his is feet. He was panting lightly as he tugged the horse aside. Adam was right on his heels and there was no time for him to catch his breath.

He caught a glimpse of his pinto and hastily went to remount the grey; determined to salvage is pride.

"You don't have to ride him, Joey." It was Jessie, her tone soft but firm. "He's my responsibility, I'll take him now."

She was standing at the great colt's head slowly stroking his face. But there was stoniness in her eyes.

Joey didn't say a word is he turned over the colt. He just took Prince's reigns and mounted him as casually as if riding the Arabian had been nothing more than a bad dream; and come to think of it wasn't really a bad dream until that last.

"Come on, horse," Jessie said firmly. "Your fathers name was Stormy Knight and your mama's name was Grey Sky; I'm going to call you Stormy Sky and you better stay out of the sky if you know it's good for you!"

"Hey, Jessie, give him a chance," Adam suggested. "I didn't see him give any indication that he might throw anyone." He finished, glancing apologetically at Joey.

Jessie's face clouded and she swung herself aboard. Her hands fitted themselves into the reigns and hauled Sky around until he was facing into the trees.

The trails were protected from the worst of the snow storms by a thick canopy of pine needles and the horses would have no real trouble keeping their footing. For six miles straight thru you could see no clear view of anything save tree branches heavy with slowly melting snow. In some places it didn't seemed as if the snow was melting at all. Like a white cave smelling of bark. They were creaking gently, as if welcoming them with their own words the trees stood sentinel; protecting them from the outside world.

They had cut these trails themselves. 'When you put your back into something you remember every detail, and it's special.' Joey's father, Chad Douglas had told them almost six years ago when they had begun the clearing.

He had helped them for the first two years and for awhile Amy, Joey's older sister, and his mother, Katie had been among them.

Jessie supposed she should be jealous of the family thing that mother and daughter did together now but, strangely, she wasn't. Instead, she was glad that they were gone now; and that the forest was theirs.

From time to time Mr. Douglas would cut some of the trees for their fireplace. But, that wasn't often and except for those times he left them alone as well.

There were at least twenty trails spiraling through the trees and Jessie, in the lead, chose the one leading the long way around the edge and then back towards her house. It met with several others, but if you stayed on, it was the longest.

There was passing room and Joey took advantage of it. He pushed Prince past Sky and took off in a fast Canter. For all his size the pony was quick. King took the signal and raced after him.

Jessie clamped her legs against Sky's barrel and followed in hot pursuit. 'When you put your back into something yourself you remember it in every detail,' and with that confidence she rode.

Claudia stopped Robert from following Jessie out. She knew the chances were good he would hover over the girl and her horse, to the point where she'd never leave the ranch.

"Robert, stay here. You, just, let her go," she said taking his arm. "The boys are there to help her and she knows how to ride."

He opened his mouth as if to protest and she cut him off. "We have other things to worry about. You know as well as I do that if Mr. Thomas decides to drop by he'll take one look at Gwen and demand you put the runt down, if not the entire litter from the looks of her."

"It would be the best thing for her," Roberts said with an oath. "She's developed an infection. I have her on medicine to help her combat it but, it's pretty severe."

"That's not what you're going to tell him," she said knowingly.

"No, I can't. Not until I'm sure that there's no hope," he said. "I know that dog. She looks like she's too weak to come through this. Really, she's just that calm of a dog. Half of the time she's lying at her master's feet. She never has been a very active dog even as a puppy. What you don't know is that her dam was destroyed a year ago last spring when she produced a litter. She didn't have many but they were big. Mike found her out in the kennel long after she'd started delivering and she was in too much distress for too long a time. I had to put her out of her pain. Gwen was the only one that survived. He raised her by hand and now he will do anything to protect her."

"It was the first time he had to go through that and it was his favorite," he continued. "He has six other breeding females. They never gave him a problem."

"What you don't know is that Gwen's was an accidental breeding as well. She's not much over a year old. Gwen was supposed to be in the house but somehow she'd managed to be out with the males. Mike is not even sure of the sire. He has two and it's anyone's guess as to which is the father. He doesn't plan to register this litter at all. There are an awful lot of breeders that would simply take best guess."

"Why doesn't he?" Claudia asked. "I would've watched them together and seen which one she took the most shine to and gone from there."

"You would but, Mike doesn't believe in chance breeding. It seems that the more you pay for a dog the higher your expectations...In some cases anyway. There are a lot of great dog owners in the show breeders' businesses. Mike Thomas is one of those," he said. "Where some other breeders will breed a female at every opportunity after her show career is over, Mike sticks to a strict schedule of one litter every other year and only then depending upon the condition of the female."

"I'm impressed," Claudia agreed. "How long has he been breeding?"

"Over ten years. I was his first Vet. He's been breeding cattle for over twenty years. He knows what he's doing and I'm not going to be able to fool him if she gets worse," he said nodding toward the clinic.

"Then get an assistant until she gets better. Use my savings," she said, firmly. "I'm too old to have much need of the money and I was going to leave it for Jessie anyway. I think that right now it would mean more to her."

"No need. She's on her way. A girl named Debby Willis. She's coming from Neenah, Wisconsin," he said. "I already have her budgeted in. We'll share rounds and I'm thinking of making her permanent in this town; someone else to take over when I'm done."

Claudia knew he meant when all the charges were brought against him and his clients started calling around for a more trustworthy Veterinarian. The thought frightened her and she stayed quiet. If the puppy lived they wouldn't be able to hide it forever.

He smiled nervously and reminded her of when he had moved back home and started the animal hospital. He had no confidence except that he was determined to be there if an animal needed him. He did his best for them and developed a reputation for himself as a conscientious man.

He had made it. He had done what was needed and as he grew older he acquired the assuredness that made him a success.

With his tall slender frame he was able to take control of the most unruly animal and owners liked that. His hands were strong and commanding, but gentle. His outspokenness made him friendships that were fast and binding. How those friendships would end had brought him back to the days of his youth. He looked boyish.

"I'll watch for him then," she told him. "If I see him coming I'll take the pup, straightaway."

"Good," he said and the boy was gone; replaced by a 43 year old man. "Gwenevere's feed is in the bag next to her kennel. I'll be back before supper. It's time I was about my rounds," he said, not knowing that she had been giving the mother extra.

Claudia smiled at him and headed for the clinic.

8
Hideout

J essie had ridden many different horses before and knew their tricks. Sky was eager to go and she waited to give him the chance. Jessie followed her friends around the last bend in the trail. Once out in the open she leaned more closely against her horse's neck and passed them like a grey shadow.

The colt shot ahead as if whipped. He wanted to be in the lead. It was as if he where in control and not Jessie and for a brief time she felt her fear returning. The speed the horse had was tremendous compared to any horse she had ever ridden before.

It was that moment of fear that kept her from turning him when the path of veered to the left. The trail was so overgrown with weeds it would be cruel to a horse even to pick your way through.

The colt was young and unfamiliar with the trail. With Jessie's slow response on the reigns; he barreled into the undergrowth and straight on into a lightly wooded area; thick with overgrown brush; that seem to stretch on for miles.

He was frightened, now, and Jessie; trying to hang on; gripped with their knees; pressing into his sides so that he was encouraged to go on. Dodging this way and that; he was trying to avoid trees that seemed to spring up out of nowhere before him.

His legs and chess were scratched and they stung. His breath became labored as he raced over the ground now strewn with a thick coat of decaying vegetation; his hooves hardly making a sound over it.

Jessie acted in desperation when she finally collected her wits and pulled back on the reins, drawing the colt in. His response to the pressure surprised her. She had to admit to herself that it was her own imagination that had earlier convinced her to be afraid of the horse. He really had done nothing to cause her fear and was only being eager.

Adam was calling her from the wood and she guessed they were trying to decide if they could risk coming in after her. Joey wouldn't. Not on Prince. Even though the brush had a fresh trail broken through it the pony wouldn't stand a chance. It was bad enough what had happened to Sky.

She'd already dismounted and was still examining the light cuts that spread from front to back on his legs. Even though he trembled he behaved well. None of the cuts were serious although without the proper care they could be. She felt guilt to wash over her. All that she had thought of irresponsible owners came back to berate her; making it even worse.

Adam couldn't go past a walk and when she looked up from Sky's injuries she found him on foot. He wouldn't even walk King through which she just raced her horse through!

"I don't' want you try to get him out, Jessie," he was saying. "Joey went to get his dad. We're going to break down the underbrush first."

"He's all cut up," Jessie said as she let her tears fall.

"I know. It's a good thing you were able to bring him under control. There's nothing worse than runaway in a field like this. Somebody's going to have to clear this out. It's too dangerous, "he said.

"Adam, you don't have to defend me. It was my fault and you know it. I knew better than to push him so soon," she said still shaken.

Adam kept silent. There was no use arguing with her in the state she was in right now. He looked around him at an old house that was standing further out in the field and decided to leave her and her horse alone as he went to investigate it.

His heavy jeans stopped most of the damage but he could still feel the grasping undergrowth try to get at him. Jessie had come pretty far into it. Another seventy five feet of weeds and he would be in the shadow of the building itself.

It was a terribly big house. The roof of its outbuilding was screwed on wrong now; making the place looked more decrepit than it really was. The frame of the house itself seems sturdy and he was just thinking it would make a great hangout when he heard Joey calling him. He gave one last long look; promising himself he would be back again. Yeah...he had plans for 'this' place! Shrugging to himself he turned his back on it for now. He really shouldn't have left Jesse at all and not for so long. The house could wait.

Jesse had stamped down a ring of the brush around Sky and had him pointing in the right direction. It was better for him if he could see who was coming at him and what they were doing as they used large shears and sickles to hack towards him. His ears were pitched forward with curiosity and he nickered nervously.

Jessie laughed and reached up a hand to stroke is face. "Silly baby," she crooned. "Don't you know a rescue when you see one?"

He nuzzled her cheek; the motion so sudden that she would have jumped back if she had had the chance. It was the look in his eyes that held her. He was looking to her for security. Two hours ago she would never have believed that right now, and from now on, she would not be able to keep herself from loving this horse. Just because of that look in his eyes. It said, 'I need you.'

"Its okay, Sky," she reassured him. "I'm right here with you and I'm going to take care of you from now on."

9
Loyalty in a Horse

Thirty eight year old Debby Willis had arrived the day after Sky. She was a pretty woman with shoulder length chestnut colored hair and her sparkling green eyes were both friendly and businesslike. She didn't make a comment about Sky's scratches but, Jessie kept her distance. She was no more than polite; wondering if the new vet blamed her as she did herself for his condition.

Debby was kind but, left Jessie to herself when she wanted to be. She answered any questions Jessie asked and took a great deal of time to care for the Dalmatians; which endeared her to Jessie.

That she loved work showed in everything she did. 'How she would handle the country veterinarian's life remain to be seen,' Jessie thought.

Anita and Margie decide to come over to see Sky two weeks after the accident; the same Saturday when Lance himself was just two weeks old.

Jesse no longer had to monitor him all the time. He was a tough little pup; a real fighter and no more had been said of putting him to sleep; and though she spent a lot of her time with him she felt she could leave him alone with Debby safely enough.

She was glad her friends were coming. She knew that Margie really had been looking forward to seeing Sky. She'd been nearly as excited about Jessie's acquisition as Jessie was. She was what most would call horse crazy and a fantastic rider.

As for Anita, well, it was a good excuse to see if Adam was over, Jessie was sure. 'Anita had never liked horses before and never thought much of riding them,' she thought wryly.

Adam did show up. The problem was that he was intent on investigating the old farmhouse that he'd had to leave so abruptly the day Sky decide to make a path to it. Skies cuts were treated and looked good as far as he was concerned. Even Anita couldn't get his attention away from the horse's condition. Jesse was watching him thoughtfully. She knew what he was going to ask before he said it and she was sure it was going to drive Anita away when she agreed to go riding with him.

Finally, he looked at her and asked, "Did your dad say you can ride him yet?"

"I've already been. Dad says it will keep him from getting stiff."

"We left the shears by the trail on our way over here," Joey said, smiling. "I've got an ax on the back of my saddle. We figured we could pull out a lot of the weeds if we used thick gloves so I took some from home."

"Are you interested?" Adam asked, the look on his face telling her that he would go alone if he had to.

"I'd love to. That is if they're going," she answered gesturing toward Anita and Margie.

To Jesses' surprise they both agreed. They thought the idea was great. 'Too bad they told them so much about the discovery at school over the past two weeks,' she thought. 'They must have made it sound too good.'

As much as she liked her friends, it seemed as if they were imposing on her own sacred grounds. It didn't leave her with any way out but, to take them with, she decided. She resigned herself to make the best of it and headed to the barn to add a saddle to Sky's back.

Joey went to bring Sky in for her when the horse took it upon himself to follow Jesse of his own accord. He stopped and watched.

"She's got him trained!" he announced, as if they could not see it for themselves. "How do you like that?"

It didn't take long to saddle and bridal Sky. He'd been trained to stand untied as he was tacked up and she did it right out in the pasture. Mounting him easily she headed out of the gate Joey held open for her.

Margie walked over to her and asked for a ride. Jessie offered Margie her stirrup and Margie swung up behind her. She was glad that sky was big for his age. They were both light and he would have no problem carrying them if she took it easy.

Anita was already on the back of the golden King by the time Jessie looked. Two people were too heavy for Prince so Joey had the privilege of riding alone.

Margie had ridden many times before but Anita was sure to give Adam a hard time. Jessie was sure she would be pulling on him for balance all the time.

Reluctantly she decided to ride behind them. That's what the buddy system was for. They could watch out for each other all the time. Besides, it was time Sky learned how to trail anyway. He did try to tug on the bit but, he didn't try to fight for the lead and she was pleased.

Adam was the only one talking on the ride to the field. All he could think about was how he wanted to clear as much of the brush as they could and, if they were able, get into the house itself by the following week. He had to think realistically when they arrived at the end of the trail and he could see again what a mountain of work was before them.

The path they'd cut to get Sky out was no more than a small strip. It was nearly impossible work compared to clearing out underbrush from between the trees. You can take that out in large clumps; this was far different. It was thickly woven and the weeds and brush were very rugged.

They worked for four hours before the sun began to give up on them and they weren't a fourth of the way through. That was with two extra hands. If Margie and Anita didn't come back to help them it would be more likely that it would take two months before they would reach the house.

They nearly had to drag Adam away. Something about that house lured him so strongly that he was willing to fight the brambles on foot again just to get there; if they would have allowed him, that is. They wouldn't.

Reluctantly he remounted his horse and pulled Anita up behind him. They left everything behind; strung up in a burlap bag and hanging in a tree. The mess of their days' labor made a puny pile on the side of the trail; seeming to mock them.

"We'll just keep on working on it until it's done," Joey said reassuringly. "It'll take some time but, you know, the old house's been there just about forever and it doesn't look like it is going anywhere."

Adam reined King about and with a determined set to his jaw rode on ahead. Even Anita left him to his thoughts; for awhile the joy would be gone from their daily rides. This was a mission of work.

Margie's mother had arrived to bring the girl's home before they got back to the Double D and they left as soon as they climbed down off the horses; making promises of coming back the next day and every weekend until the job was done. It seemed to lighten Adam's mood a little and the boys rode off for home at a brisk trot.

Jessie put Sky up for the night and was laughing to her self about how suddenly Adam had found a purpose in life. She gave Sky a final pat; made a silent prayer that the weather would hold for Adams' sake; and headed in to check on Lancelot.

10
Lancelot

She sat next to the kennel and cried quietly. Mike Thomas, the selfish killer, had taken Gwen home. He'd be lucky if he didn't have to bring her right back, anyway.

Worst of all, her father had agreed that Mr. Thomas had just as good of a chance of tending to her as he did!

Her throat was stuck tight and dry. Her father didn't have to tell her that Mr. Thomas had put Lance down. She watched Mr. Thomas leave with the pups and Lancelot was not among them.

A long time ago she thought she had braced herself for this day; only to find out that you never can brace yourself at all.

She would be anything else but she would never be able to do what her father had just done. She couldn't be that kind of Vet; she couldn't be a Vet at all. A lawyer could lose a case and it might be his fault; a teacher might have to fail a student if he did badly in class, and it might be just what the student needed to learn better; but there was no way that she would be able to tell someone that their pet had to die.

From now on; she was determined to stay as far away from her Fathers' work as possible; completely if she could.

The following Saturday was not just warm and slushy from melt, it was raining. They were ankle deep in mud with frozen ground underneath.

They didn't stand a chance taking the horses up the hill to cut thru the woods. Riding along the road was safer but, it took an hour longer.

Adam was surprised that Jessie was still willing to go at all. Even he expected her to be locked in her room; mourning the loss of her pup. But, she seemed as eager to return to the house as he was.

She wasn't quiet either. Where their rides were usually one sided, with him doing the talking, it was Jessie now; and she kept the conversation away from Lance as neatly as she hid her feelings on his death.

Sky was groomed to within an inch of his life and the care she took with his coat was almost as obsessive as the care she took when it came to riding him. He looked fantastic.

No more wild gallops now it was a gentle trot or canter whether he liked it or not. And he didn't like it one bit. It was a good thing the colt liked her or he would have bolted away by now. Adam was not going to make her hurry just because the trail was bad. He knew better.

When the house finally came into view the three of them groaned in unison. Everything they had cut and set aside had sluiced its way back to the path they had carved. It looked puny; like they had done nothing at all.

"Are you going to just give up?" Jessie asked Joey as he sat on Prince.

"I just think we should wait until spring when it dries up a bit," he answered. "It doesn't make sense to kill our selves over this. I mean it's been here for years and we haven't bothered it until now. It can wait. I know he's on some kind of wish quest but, we don't have to be," he said, pointing at Adam who was lugging the sodden weeds back in the woods. "It's practically a river that he's standing in."

"If you're afraid to get your feet wet, that's fine with me. On the other hand I have nothing better to do," Jessie said.

"You two don't have any sense left in your heads," Joey said. "Go on then and I hope you both come down sick."

He reined Prince back thru the off side of the woods towards his house and Adam shrugged, dismissing him.

"How rude; he didn't even a say goodbye. It looks like we can count on him as much as we counted on Anita and Margie," Jessie said when Joey was out of hearing.

She dismounted and began to work. As long as she kept her mind on other things she could avoid what plagued her. Joey's unwillingness to help didn't matter at all. She could forgive him. It was her father she would not forgive. He'd not even allowed her to say goodbye to Lance and, unlike Joey, she would never see 'him' again.

Aunt Claudia didn't stop Jessie from riding off every weekend to work on the new trail. It had kept her out of the house for more than three weeks and that was as much what she needed as Jessie did. Not that she wanted her gone all the time. She knew she had to let Jessie deal with her grief the only way that she knew how; and for awhile at least; she needed her gone.

His spots were neatly spread out on his glossy white coat. Just a hint of them but, 'Jessie would barely recognize him now,' Claudia mused as she stroked the Dalmatian puppy in her lap.

He had just finished his afternoon feeding and was fast asleep again. Something he still did most of the time. Claudia kept the puppy tucked into her bottom drawer most of the nights. When she knew that her brother and his assistant were going to be out for the day he resided on the kitchen floor or in the cupboard under the sink; if he were napping. The drawer was deep and for now it would keep him in but, it worried her that latter she would have to devise a way of penning him.

She called him Lance. When he had to go back to his owner it wouldn't matter, he would still be Lance to Jessie and to her as well. He was a quiet little thing, mostly, and she had to keep him that way. She had to remind herself to speak his name softly to him if Jessie where at home.

For three weeks she had kept her vigil; pacing herself and him to regular feedings; cleaning out his bed when she woke in the morning and again at night. At five weeks old he was getting pretty big.

She knew he was out of danger now. He had made it. Someday this spotted runt would be a dog; as long as she kept him here. It was far too soon to inform Mike Thomas of what she'd done and she just wasn't up to it.

Robert had taken it as almost a relief when she told him the pup, at last, had died. He knew that sometimes it was just too much to expect when a pup was born so small.

"He must have developed a respiratory problem. He hadn't been well since you left this morning. Debby was out on rounds and I could not reach you," she had told him; the practiced lie falling easily from her lips.

Robert had said it would be better if Mr. Thomas could take the others then. Better for Jessie. She wouldn't have to be reminded of Lance by his litter mates being there.

"Mr. Thomason had already called Debby this morning; asking if he could take his pets home and he would be happy to hear, now, that he could."

That was the last Robert had really spoken about it. He'd sent Debby to Petersburg on a few occasions and dropped by himself when he had the chance. Gwenevere and the rest of the pups were all doing well.

Hearing voices outside, Claudia hastily put Lance back in his drawer and went back downstairs. She actually felt better with all the extra exercise she was getting. Her arthritis wasn't nearly as bad as it normally was this time of year.

'I could never be as active as those kids have been lately,' she thought.

Now that the sun was in the skies later at night they were gone as soon as Jessie finished her chores and didn't come back for hours.

She was leery of letting Jessie mess around with that old farmhouse. If things hadn't been so hard on Jessie lately she never would have agreed to let her go there. At least she had her friend Margie and the boys with her so that she wasn't alone. Funny; how happy Jessie had been when Anita Whitman had begged out of the work.

She entered the kitchen and looked out the window. Jessie must still be in the barn tending to Sky. It was wonderful how the horse had taken to her. He demanded her attention and thankfully Jessie didn't resent it. Instead she was happy to cater to him.

He may not have been the first thing Jessie had fallen for but, he had kept her heart open when it surely would have been slammed shut to any other.

Claudia began finishing her cooking in earnest. It looked better if it seemed that she had been busy instead of having everything on simmer. She was very much looking forward to the day when she would tell them all just how busy she had been so that the extra work was over but, she was afraid of it as well.

Jessie breezed into the kitchen in triumph. They'd made it thru the underbrush and had spent the day foraging in the building itself.

"You wouldn't believe it, Auntie! Its chuck full of antiques!" she gushed. "I mean they're not in the best of condition…but, some of the stuff they used to have!"

"I'm surprised there's anything left," Claudia said. "They had an auction when the people moved out of there, oh, must be twenty five years ago."

"Has dad found out who owns it yet?" Jessie asked excitedly. I mean it's considered abandoned isn't it."

"It's owned by the county," her Aunt answered. "It's abandoned all right. The old man who owned it passed away and the people who rented it from him moved on after that. How much did they leave behind?"

"Tons! He must have been a pack rat," Jessie laughed. "We're going to leave it there. You wouldn't believe it but Margie is decorating. Cleaning house you might say. It's great!"

Claudia chuckled. "I think I wish I was up to coming with you. Is the drive over long?"

"Yeah, it's pretty bad right now. I think we might as well take the time to clear that out as well."

"Not yet. It's the opposite direction from the way you come and I'll let you have your fun before I start nosing around," Claudia said. "I have your dinner ready."

Jessie settled into her chair and was fairly slopping her supper onto her plate before her Aunt admonished her for it.

"Settle down, Jessie. You're making a mess of it. Here let me," she said, "you have a one track mind."

"I wish I did, Auntie," Jessie said, tiredly. "I'm trying....to not think of Lance but, you know, I swear sometimes I can hear him crying. And I've been having these awful dreams. Nightmares where I find him and others like him and they're out there, and Auntie, they're all alone."

She pushed her uneaten dinner away and the tears rolled down her face in slow rivulets. She wasn't trying to stop them this time. She just let them fall.

Claudia nearly told her then but didn't. This wouldn't be the way for it to happen. Jessie's happiness at knowing Lance was alive would be crushed too quickly if Robert didn't get his anger out first and that would have to happen privately; without Jessie. She had lied to him about the puppies' death and even though he couldn't take the blame on himself he would be loath to allow her to.

Besides, he very well might want to give the pup back to Mike and not even tell Jessie. She had already experienced the death of the pup; far better than watching him slowly waste away. There had been a very real chance of that and it was one of the reasons that Claudia had taken Lancelot away in the first place. The other was that she was not going to allow him to destroy his career. Jessie would have to wait to know about the pup based on the results of her conversation with Robert and that was that!

'Oh, what a fool she had been,' she thought, 'an old fool! Of course Jessie had to have heard his whimpers. It was not so quiet at night when the large house echoed every sound.'

"I understand bad dreams, Jessie," Claudia began, "I've had them myself. Lance isn't lost and we wouldn't be able to find all of the wayward pets that are out there. It takes time but, you will stop having them, mostly. You can't make yourself forget overnight. If you did it would be as if he never mattered to you."

"Maybe you're trying too hard. You're not giving yourself a chance to think about it; to put in its proper place so to speak. Try to remember that they're a lot of dogs out there that need someone even more than Lance did. He has seven litter mates that are doing wonderful," she said. "I understand that Mr. Thomas intends to give them away."

Jessie's eyes widened and she brushed away the tears. "If you think I'm going to just run right over there and beg one of them from him to take Lance's place you're wrong, Auntie. I don't ever want another dog!"

"He didn't have anything to do with Lance, Jessie. You know that," Claudia said.

"It doesn't matter does it? If things had been different and Mr. Thomas had told dad to spare no expense to save him; no matter what the cost, I think dad would've done it. I think he would have hired Debby to watch over him around the clock just so that he could be here now. But, he wanted him dead and dad was glad when he did die!"

"No he wasn't," Claudia said giving Jessie a level look. "Every time one of his charges dies he considers himself a failure. Even though it's not his fault. I know he does everything he can to save them. He wishes he could perform the same miracles that you expect of him. If he didn't he never would have tried to save Lance in the first place."

"Think about it, Jessie. Think about why you want to be angry at someone because you're hurting. It's not right you lashing out like that. Find something that you want and work towards it instead. It's time that you start to pull out the best of this world instead of dwelling on the worst! And, before you start to think that I don't care what you're going through, remember that I love you."

"I know, Auntie," Jesse said softly. "I'm trying."

"Good. Your father will be home soon and if you don't want him to see you like this you should chin up and eat your dinner," she said firmly.

Jessie pulled her plate back and began eating but, the bites she took were small and few between.

Roberts' boots clumping down in the entryway made both of them jump. They'd been so caught up talking that they never heard his truck pull in.

Jessie glanced in his direction and all of her arguments vanished. He was smiling and led in a thick coated mongrel that stood about as tall as his knees. It didn't resemble any dog that she knew of. He was nearly all white but, so filthy and matted it was hard to tell what he was supposed to look like.

"You want to ride with me, Jessie? I've found the Skinners' dog," he said happily. It seems he's done quite well for him self. He's twice the size he was when he strayed off last summer. Hard to imagine a dog could pack on so much in just five months but, I think the kids will like him back just as well."

"Yeah, I'll come," Jessie answered. Jessie was told about the missing dog. Two of the kids that own him had been on about him missing every day at school. Although they were all keeping an eye out for him, not a trace of him had been found and they had pretty much given up.

She'd gotten to her feet and was walking over to the mutt when his teeth went back and he growled. She stopped dead still. In the small kitchen there was barely enough room to turn around and she allowed that if she did manage to get that far he'd have her by the time she reached the door.

Robert MacMurray was obviously taken aback by the dogs' actions. He brought the dog into the truck and home with no problem at all. He looked wretched now but, Robert had known him for a friendly, playful dog at home with his family.

His owner kept all the shots current. It wasn't the medicine. A dog with rabies would have shown some indications that he had the disease. And here he was, faced with a dog that looked for all the world like he wanted to eat his daughter alive.

He moved slowly; patting his shin and calling coaxingly, "hey Skipper. Come here, boy. There's a good dog. You want a treat? Common…"

"He backed gradually towards the back door hoping that he might call the mutt back outside and away, but the dogs blazing eyes never left Jessie. With the click of the door handle the friendly mutt named Skipper charged.

Jessie followed the movement of the animal as it collected itself and bolted. The hall seemed miles long as she ran. There was only one room where she could shut the door behind her and as she reached the clinic and stopped to open it her back was seared with the red hot pain of a bite.

She fell forward into the room and landed on her chin; the blow knocking her teeth together in rending pain. Her senses went fuzzy and she found she didn't have the strength to fight back.

Robert wrestled the dog from his daughter and watched her eyes close. He had the foresight to grab the dogs muzzle and he lifted up and back. With a vicious thrust forward the dog was kenneled. The gate slammed shut down its' prisoner before the animal could even turn around. It had lost its chance. In its fury it rent its teeth on the links of the cage.

"Hell dog," Robert panted; his shock freezing him where he was. He was drained with fear. No mad dog in his life looked like this one. No book he'd ever read prepared him for the hate issuing in waves from this beast. "My god, what have you become?"

"Robert!" Claudia screamed. "Robert she's unconscious!" He turned and knelt at his daughters' side in one graceful motion regaining himself as he did. His panic gone as swiftly as it had come replaced by a fierce determination.

The back of Jessie's blouse was bloody but not so much it would cause her to blackout. His mind echoed the sound of her head hitting the floor and raced with the options open to him now.

In the truck he could get her to the hospital in twenty minutes; much faster than waiting for an ambulance from town. He had already risked her life once tonight and had to dare himself to do once again.

He rolled her gently on her back as he supported her head in his hand. He winced with how small she looked to him. He'd decided instantly to take her to town himself.

Skipper, still raging in his kennel; began throwing himself against the gate. His paws slamming against the tile floor as he fought for traction.

Somewhere over the din Robert heard a car pull in. The animal might get out of the kennel if he pushed hard enough at the bottom and wriggled under. If he did there was only one way to hold him back and that was lock him behind the clinic door.

He got to his feet and stooped to lift Jessie, hoping fervently that her neck wasn't injured.

"Shut that tight!" he said to Claudia as she followed. "I need a blanket and get yourself a coat. You have to come with me. When I come back here it will be with a gun," he snarled.

Debby pulled her shoes back on as soon as she saw Jessie in her Fathers' arms. "I'll drive," she said quickly. "Let me get my car around."

"She raced out of the house; leaving him standing there. He heard his sisters' footsteps above him as she gathered the things he requested.

It seemed so slow. How many minutes? How long had it been since he had seen Jessie smiling at him just before the attack? The enormity of what had happened made it seem forever; and in another room a dog raged; wanting more.

11
What Jessie Needs Most

Robert held Jesse in the back seat. She was wrapped in one of the blankets Claudia had brought down. It didn't occur to him to ask her why she brought another and had it messed in her lap.

Only Debby saw Claudia pull the blanket back from the spotted puppy. As she drove she kept glancing at the old woman gently stroking the passive Dalmatian. She marveled at the strength she had to have; bringing down such a heavy burden so quickly and the calmness she showed as she sat next to her keeping the pup from her brothers' view.

Claudia answered with a crooked smile. Her explanation would have to wait. For right now the pup would have to wait for Jessie...as she had to wait for him. 'All questions were on hold,' was what that smile said.

The lights of the small hospital glowed welcomely before them and Claudia hastily put the blanket back over her charge. His curiosity had been piqued when they had entered the car. The only thing that kept him from causing a disturbance was the familiar hands that stroked him. As the car settled into its' slot he began to struggle.

"I'm going to find us rooms at the hotel, Robert," Debby began, "and I think I'll call Max. Just in case. We'll don't want him walking into the house right now."

"Good. I'm sorry I didn't think of it myself. While you're at it call the Sheriff for me. I'm going to let him take care of this one."

Two attendants came out to the car and he told them what had happened. They hastened to get a stretcher and he eased himself out of the car to let them have room.

Robert didn't stay to watch them off, not surprised when Claudia made no effort to leave the car. She would come back with Debby and he was sure it would be soon.

The small hospital was well staffed. Though accustomed to the types of injuries incurred by farm animals and machinery; their only questions regarded the types of injuries that Jessie had sustained and not how or why she'd gotten them. Those questions were sure to come as soon as they had done their best for her and he knew that they would be many. Guilt washed over him again.

They rushed her into a room and away from him before he had a chance to ask if he could follow, leaving him at the front desk with Mrs. West, the receptionist.

"Doctor Leigh has everything under control, Mr. MacMurray," she offered, smiling with understanding. "Why don't you come and have a sit over here while you wait. We'll get her all registered and before you know it they'll be done."

"Grudgingly, he took the chair offered and though his gaze wandered freely towards the emergency room he answered all the questions put to him as though running items for a list of medical inventory; flat and calm while inside he roiled with all the possibilities. For once he felt plum useless.

12

Other People's Dogs

Claudia stayed in the car with Debby when she left. She was smart enough to know a good rescue when she saw one. Debby could have called from the hospital more easily than driving to the hotel right away. The proprietors of the hotel where friends and their doors were always open. They had plenty of time to register.

"Why did you bring him?" Debby asked when they were on their way. "From the looks of him it wouldn't have done him harm to go the night without you."

"For Jessie," she said simply.

"She knows about him?"

"Not yet," Claudia answered, "after what's happened I don't know how she'll feel knowing. But, she needs him. You haven't heard him at night because your room is too far down the hall. It seems he's been the cause of a number of nightmares. She's been having them for a long time now but I didn't know about them until just before Robert brought that...,"she sniffed harshly and continued, "that beast home."

"He's a monster...a freak! In all my years I've never ever heard of a dog doing what he did. When Robert led him in he

LISA VANDERLEEST

looked as friendly as you please. It just went berserk so sudden! There was no warning at all! Poor Robert…I don't know if he'll ever be able forgive himself."

Debby stopped her car and went around to help Claudia carry the blankets. "There's a little leash in the glove if you want to try to coax him to relieve himself."

"He stays by me," Claudia responded setting the pup in the driest part of the lawn she could find. He tucked his tail immediately and rolled his dark brown eyes at them.

"Turn your head," Claudia said, "he's shy." Debby did and said, "He's grown up quite a bit. It's hard to believe he's from the same litter but, he hasn't been in any danger for quite a while."

"No, but I have. I know there's no chance that he'll be destroyed now. It's the timing that's been all wrong; for everyone, including me," she said picking him up again. "When Mr. Thomas finds out I don't think he's going to be too keen on our keeping him. I'm not even sure he won't accuse Robert of plotting the whole thing."

"He's a kind man, Claudia," Debby said, "but; I'm not going to tell you that I know how he's going to react to this. I just wish you would have told me what you were up to so that could help too."

Claudia looked at her in astonishment, her mouth agape. "Oh, I would've probably tried to stop you…just not real hard. He was doing well when he died…uh, when you abducted him."

"For a long time I worried over what had caused him to take such a turn for the worst. As a matter of fact, I had run myself pretty ragged chasing out to Mr. Thomas's ranch worrying that the same sickness that had brought down that pup might affect the others. A mystery disease if you will. You might have saved me."

80

The hotel was really no more than a rooming house. When they entered and told the story to the owners; they were willing to let them stay pup and all.

When Jessie awoke it was with a dull burning pain between her shoulders. It took her a while to remember what had caused it but, when she did she sat up stiffly and searched the room as if expecting to be attacked again. Her body wasn't ready for such motion and she was rewarded with a quick headache. She lay back slowly and rubbed at it weakly.

From the hall she made out the voice of her father talking to the doctor. It seemed she would live. They were not talking about her at all. The conversation revolved around some trouble the farmers were having with their sheep. She closed her eyes again deciding to resume her nap.

Debby's full attention was on the conversation going on between her boss and the doctor. Robert had already had the Sheriff out to the house and Skipper was no more. He had done an autopsy and tested to determine if the dog was rabid.

What they found out was for the most part satisfying. The dog was not rabid and the loss of sheep from the surrounding community seemed to be solved.

You don't call the Vet for dead sheep if they were killed by an attacker but, they had heard of the large number that had died from the authorities and they had made numerous trips to some of the farms to confirm the cause of death. It was dogs or wolves. Which were the scavengers and which the killers had until now been undetermined.

"It must have been him. He was vicious. A killer if I ever saw one and I never came across one like this in all my life," Robert was saying. "I can't figure out why he took to it when he was so well taken care of at home. But his type of herding is over."

"Is that what you think made him attack your daughter," the doctor asked, "his lust to kill?"

"Or the tight quarters after having been caught," the Sheriff said.

"No, that dog looked like hate itself," Robert replied. "No dog would attack that fiercely unless it had practice."

"I don't want Jessie leaving the house," Debby said quickly. "She can exercise her horse in the field and I'll watch her," she added.

"There's no reason for that is there?" Doctor Leigh asked, his Asian accent sounding thicker with emotion as he spoke to her. "We don't want her to be frightened of her own shadow, now do we? The damage is done. I think the best thing for her would be to try to get back to normal."

"Not in this case, I'm afraid," she said, vehemently. She gestured them out of the hall and into a private room where she continued. "The last two places I had been to didn't show the prints of one dog. Unless every dog in these parts all of a sudden decided to take up foraging for themselves," she said. "I counted at least six extra sets; and with the way they were intermixed; I think there might be more."

"A dog pack!" Claudia said shocked. "You think they might go after people!"

"It's happened before," Robert mused. "Not that Debby expects it to happen here, I think, but, if there's a chance I think we'd better spread the word."

"And set up a search party," doctor Leigh added. "Your daughter was lucky. She's got one nasty bite and a slight concussion. It's a good thing you reacted quickly. Her jaws going to give her a hard time for a while but, if you hadn't latched on to him when you did my stitching job could have been much harder. Personally I don't want to have to do this assembly line style. No one else gets hurt."

"No one else has reported their dogs missing," Robert said. "I asked the Sheriff. Let's not go overboard. I'd like to do a little investigating before we put together a search party. Let's find out who's been leaving their dogs run at night."

"It might not be the local dogs," Claudia interjected, "years back we had a problem like this; long before you were born, Robert. No people were hurt, though, just some sheep and small animals."

"I remember my dad telling me about that," Sheriff Hill said. "The men found them, all right. They were stray dogs dumped off here from Ruthford. The city folk didn't have a pound back then so they set them loose to live on their own out here; maybe hoping that some farmer would take them in."

Claudia took a seat in one of the chairs in the room before going on. They joined her and she smiled thankfully. 'It was hard getting old,' she thought, knowing she was only stiff from tending Lancelot.

"There were ten of them; all kinds," she continued. "When they where brought in they where so battle scarred it seemed they must have been out there forever. And I suppose they were; before anyone knew they where there."

"The Skinners dog had over a dozen healing wounds and several open ones," Debby said. "He'd only been missing since summer."

"Oh. Well, then they're scrappers when they take a notion to go wild," Claudia said. "They did a good job on the sheep, though. Every Farmer in these parts lost at least one sheep, so they're roamers too."

Robert got to his feet and went to the door. He stopped with his hand on the knob and his head down, con-templating. The three of them looked at him silently and waited. Finally he turned to them and his eyes were moist in his strained face. "Jessie stays home and no one tells her why," he said thickly. "She has had it hard enough with losing her dog. I don't want her terrorized. I should have raised her in the city," he said, before leaving the room, "she was right all along."

Robert entered Jessie's room quietly and was happy to find her still asleep. There was an ugly bruise that covered the left side of her jaw and a mark on her chin that was as vivid as strawberry juice; that she wouldn't be too pleased with; but, he was just relieved that she was going to be all right. The bite wounds were small and would not have been much of a problem. It was the dog driving her to the floor that had caused her long hospital visit.

He sat next to her bed and took her hand and she stirred, waking to look at him bleary from a sleep no different from a normal morning wakeup call. She had lost her fright.

The Harris children had been happy to entertain Lancelot. They were friendly kids; ranging in age from five to eleven. It seemed a pure pleasure to them to live at the motel with their parents. The eleven year old was a sturdy boy named Steven and he had proudly announced that he had been 'personally' in charge of the pup all morning and had done a good job, 'thank you'.

Claudia laughed and took out her wallet. She had promised him a dollar to do the job and reached in for three. Five year old Joshua wouldn't know how to spend his any more than his seven year old sister Beverly but, she supposed an ice cream each would probably take care of it.

None of that mattered to Lance. His dark brown eyes were shining up at her as his tongue lolled haphazardly out of the side of his mouth. They had kept him bouncing around so hard he was panting.

She handed the children their dollars and lifted him up from among them. Immediately he was in her arms he began to cover her face was sloppy kisses of gratitude.

They said their 'goodbyes' and 'thank yous' to Ms. Harris, collected their things, and left.

"You have to tell him now. You know that," Debby said in the car. "There's no more waiting for the right time."

"That's why you're taking me to the hospital," Claudia said quietly.

"You can't bring him in there! If his mind wasn't on Jessie and the fact that you were in a dark car with heavy blankets covering him; and I still don't know how you pulled that off so well; let me remind you that you'd still have to get him past the hospital nurses and doctors!"

"But, I'll have you riding shotgun," Claudia laughed.

"No way," Debby answered, starting the car. "We're going home!"

Claudia reached over and held the shift lever in place. Her smile faded and in its place was the hardness of years of labor and with it the patient and experience. "I don't care if they catch me. What are they going to do with a fifty year old woman? Haul me away in chains? That girl has gone through enough to hate, or at least, fear dogs for the rest of her life and here sits the cure!"

Debby stroked the small spotted head. He turned his face and began methodically washing her wrists. A moment later she quietly took her hand away and putting the car in gear, headed for the hospital.

13
Spots and All

ebby had held up her end of the bargain as smoothly as a thief. Going on ahead of her and diverting Mrs. West's attention long enough for Claudia to pass through the hallway and into Jessie's room.

Robert had gone home with the Sheriff to make his calls and collect his truck. He wouldn't be back for quite some time and, if the nurses decided to leave them to themselves, she might just have time to explain to Jessie why she had allowed her to go through so much grief.

The hospital was too small for a private room but, it didn't have a lot of patients either. Jessie was alone in a room with two beds, sitting up when her aunt entered; her face storming back at her; with such anger that for a moment Claudia was taken aback.

"You can take it right back," she hissed, thru clenched teeth. "I told you that I didn't want one of those pups and I meant every word of it!"

"Oh, Jessie, you're wrong. It's Lancelot!" Claudia gasped. Jesse's mouth dropped open and for a time she just looked back at her Aunt in astonishment. It quickly snapped shut again when her aunt tried to come to her.

She searched the spotted body hoping for something that might give him away; half hoping that it wasn't a lie. But what she saw was an animal that looked nothing like the one she knew. If she were to go to look over his entire litter with this one back his place, she would not be able pick him out again, and her Aunt knew it.

"I want to be alone please," she whispered, "just take it away. I don't want it." She rolled over on her side and pulled the blanket up around her shoulders. The last thing she wanted to look at was another dog. She'd had enough of them to last a lifetime.

Claudia reached over and placed the pup on the bed and walked over to a chair in the corner. She sat down and began telling Jessie, how she, and then everyone else had been duped into believing he was dead. As she did the pup was fervently trying to nuzzle the only companion left to him.

About halfway into her explanation, Jessie slid the covers out from under Lance and drew him to her. The motions of her petting him showing through them.

"If you want to go and see the rest of them and take a count," Claudia said when she finished her story, well you'd see that they're all a much different size and the rest of them are all still there…"

"I know it's him," Jessie said simply. "There's something special he has, it's just in his right ear. I had forgotten it but, he just showed it to me. It's his luck charm you see? He was born with one spot and it looked like a little piece of dirt when he was born; and I used it to wish on it. To wish he would live. You saved my puppy for me, Auntie," she added in a whisper.

"Then I'll leave you alone with him for a while, okay," Claudia said quietly as she got to her feet. "Just for a little while. Debby has been holding Mrs. West at bay enough and I'll have to bring him home soon.

"Thank you, auntie," Jesse said as the door softly closed.

14
He's Yours

Robert hustled Lancelot straight off to Petersburg, without saying anything to Claudia or Debby about the conspiracy but, instead, taking them with so that they could see what trouble they had caused.

Mr. Thomas's reaction to news that his pup was alive surprised them all. He laughed until tears came when Robert confessed what had been done.

"It sounds like something my own mother would do," he laughed. "She came home with a kitten one day and my father would have none of it. He hated them. For no reason, mind you. He just did, and he told her to bring it back straight off. Next time you saw that kitten it was almost a cat. She'd gone and kept it in any room that he wasn't in and when it finally made its debut it had sneaked in on him while he slept in his favorite chair. Cat's like comfort and this one curled up under his chin and slept with him!" he laughed again and continued, "My dad woke up and was looking straight into the face of that tigers golden eyes. Well, I tell you, no one was sadder when twelve years later, dad's cat finally passed away. I hope your Jessie's pup lives that longer or older!"

Jessie came home at the end of the week. They'd kept her in the hospital for three days. Although she felt fine and was awake for most of the time, the doctor wanted to be sure that her head injury didn't amount to more than it appeared. When he was satisfied he sent her off with the firm orders that she was to get several days rest and then only cautiously venture out. If school was too much she was to do her studies at home.

Holding the sleeping pup firmly on her lap she sat in front of the fireplace, wishing fervently that she could be out. The house seemed haunted with its steady creaks and groans and with only Aunt Claudia to keep her company. She wanted nothing more than to be back off of her imposed vacation.

Out the window she could see Sky and his anxious play in his pasture. He seemed as restless as she was. Even more with the melting snow smelling so clean and fresh with spring. She watched as he tossed his head and called out with his bugling whinny, let's go!

Her jaw still ached and she had developed a habit of rubbing it. She moved her hand from Lance and he woke, immediately expecting to be let down. Letting him go she went once again to plead her case to her Aunt.

She wasn't using words anymore as they had gotten her nowhere. Her tactics were simply to be as much under foot as she could. If she proved too much of a nuisance, she supposed she would be kicked out, long before her confinement was supposed to end. It had worked before when she had been sick. The only problem this time was that they weren't telling her a few days and she could go out, this time they weren't telling her when she could go out at all.

When her aunt was in the laundry she pested her with questions that were as silly as a child's. In the kitchen she botched every task she was given and while Claudia had gotten in the habit of watching her daily soaps, she turned them off when Jessie's groans of displeasure interrupted them so often that she was completely lost as to what was happening in them. She had even managed to be banned from dusting when she dropped one of her fathers' favorite vases. The only thing that kept it from bursting into a million shards was the thickness of the carpet. And when they argued about music the radio was silenced as well.

To all her objectives she had been unsuccessful. She would resort to begging.

Aunt Claudia cast Jessie a surly look when she entered the kitchen and sat down to watch her chopping vegetables into bits and pieces. Jessie pouted back at her.

"Can I go see Sky?" she asked. "He's out there all alone and no one is there to visit him."

"No," Claudia said without a pause, "and you know you can't."

"He's going crazy out there! If he doesn't get ridden pretty soon he's liable to throw me when you do let me!"

"Well, if he does then you dad will be justified in selling him. Besides, that's a poor excuse. Sky wouldn't throw you and you know it as well as I do," her Aunt said, nonchalantly.

"I can't help it. I need to get out! Max could use my help… You said so yourself that I shouldn't be letting him do all of work. I could take it easy," she said, letting a note of desperation creep into her voice.

"Not a chance, Jessie, doctor's orders and that's that," she answered.

She stopped mincing and regarded Jesse with their hands on our hips. "You couldn't even then. Your father's decided to put a stop to your wanderings. You're not allowed out of the pasture on Sky and you'll have to be in the house when you're not riding him. So you'd better get tame real fast."

"You can't mean that. I haven't done anything wrong!" she shouted at her.

"I didn't say that you did," Claudia answered, gently. "It's for your own safety. If you'd come across that dog out there alone you would've had no way to get yourself help, and that won't do. We just never thought about that before, that's all. What if you did take a fall from your horse? Who would be there to bring your home?"

Jesse didn't take time to think about it. She stared at her aunt with all the fury of a caged animal.

"Joey and Adam! Or maybe Max...I haven't been in trouble for thirteen years and now when I'm older..."

"And while they chase all over looking for you, you could be lying somewhere waiting. Better to go on the buddy system. Have them come here to get you. But I'm not sure that you can talk your father into letting you go to that old farmhouse anymore; not at least until he's had a chance to look it over himself."

"So I'm just stuck here now! One time I get hurt in my life and just like that I have to be punished! It's not fair!"

"You'll have to take it up with him but, I'll tell you that I'm on his side and so are Debby and your doctor," she said, resuming her chore. "It will do you no good to get all put out about it. You can ride here or where you can be seen from the road. Now stop causing me grief. You never were so clumsy when you were little either and if that's any indication of how careful you would be it makes me more convinced you're staying put. Sky won't have to throw you with the way you've been lately; you'd fall off if he was standing still."

Jessie bit her lip. She had gone too far already by blowing up at her Aunt the way she had. Regretting it now she apologized, and shifted the conversation back to Sky.

"Can I at least go and see him?" she asked weakly. "I only want to pat him."

Her aunt consented and she went outside to muddle out the situation by herself.

Robert was riding a dull black horse of vintage age shown by his nearly white muzzle. He had retired D'Mico three years ago and only took him for a short ride about twice a week for the exercise. He was just a pet now.

The gelding was so steady that he could have a rifle shot from his back and the animal night might not even start. For over three months Robert had led riding parties on him in search of the killers.

On several farms they had come across tracks and once the remains of a young calf. The prints told them the grisly story as clearly as if they had spoken to them. The wolves were only scavenging...The killers were dogs of various sizes; and none of them small.

Whether they were masters of illusion or just plain lucky, it didn't matter. Each time the riders had followed the tracks, even in fresh mud, they would abruptly disappear into a stream or thick brush.

Then the party would head back in and plan out the next days' course. Early May flowers were in full bloom and those killers were still out in the fields mocking them.

When Lance was still small Jessie tried in vain to keep him away from Sky's dancing hooves. But, Dalmatians are coach dogs and something about the breed gives them an affinity with horses un-bested by any other.

Lance was no exception. He delighted in the horse and, as Dalmatians also grow quickly, it was no time at all when he was bounding under Sky's belly and between his hooves, as confident as if he were born there. At four months he had lost most of his early potbelly and was trim with not much to spare. And he was bursting with high energy.

He trained so easily that only a cross word was enough to rebuke him when he made a mistake; and Jessie spent hours teaching him to fetch, roll over, and any other silly trick that might come to her.

These talents he proudly displayed whenever guests would visit. But, when called on to perform simple obedience he would throw all manners aside and be as unruly as he pleased. When called to heel he would run off and play chase. He would sit long enough to touch bottom and then be right back on his feet.

"Patience, Jessie," her father, admonished. "He's still a pup at heart and he will come around and time."

"He just doesn't want to do it and I can't seem to make him want to. He'd rather goof off than have a treat for doing what he is supposed to. He knows what I want from him," she complained.

"I think you're right. He does," he agreed. "But, he's restless. It's going to be awhile before he burns off his youthful energy. Take when you ride; he comes in all worn out. He sleeps it off and is ready to go as soon as he wakes up. Go slower when you're out and don't tucker him so much. Then you might be able to work with him better," he suggested.

"It's being confined to such a small area," Jessie said. "If I could take him for a walk…"

"Well, you can't and you'll have to make do with what you have. I'm going on my rounds," he offered, "you could get out by coming with me?"

"No thanks," she grumbled. "I think I'll stay here were I belong. Do you want to tie me up?"

"No, the next thing you'd be teaching him is the rope chewing trick," he said shaking his head as he left.

15

A Sense of Freedom

She watched the truck pull way in anticipation. Her aunt had taken the day to visit with friends and Debby was already out of town on rounds. It was the only day that she had been left completely alone since she'd been bitten and she waited only long enough for the truck to be out of sight. When it disappeared under the trees she raced for Sky's saddle and she had him ready to go in no time. He had already been groomed first thing in the morning.

As she rode off she was pleased that things were going so well. With Lance in tow she headed for the woods.

In her eagerness to see how far the boys had gotten on the house she had let Sky have his head and he bounded off in a quick canter. If Joey and Adam weren't there now they soon would be.

They hadn't missed a Saturday since they had first started going there and every Monday they told her of their new finds.

She rode up to the back of the house fifteen minutes later and threw herself off of Sky's back. All the overgrowth around the house was gone and taking her horse by the reigns she led him toward the front.

It didn't surprise her when she didn't see the boy's mounts. It was early and she would rather that they wouldn't show up until she had some time to go over things herself. She tied Sky to a small tree in the front of the house and entered it.

The first thing she noticed was the smell. It smelled like the clinic when dogs were kept there. The next were the paw prints on the floor. The mud of them was beginning to dry but, they were moist enough to have been put down very recently.

The back door had been shut when she rode up. She was sure of that much. But when she'd come up the rickety stair at the front, that door had been swinging in the breeze, and the paw prints marched through it as if there had been a parade.

On the table in the first room were candy and several wrapped sandwiches. No one had touched them yet.

She began backing out of the house. The boys had already been there and they'd left again in a hurry.

Lance's yelp spun her round and she flew to the door, not a second before he raced through it. He'd been bitten but, his pursuer had lost interest in him when it caught sight of Sky.

Her heart caught in her throat as she watched Sky lashing at the dogs, his screams peeling out in fear. He reared and his head twisted back and forth against the bridal that held him. His legs thrust out at his enemies sending them back but, they kept on at him.

Sweat began to darken his coat and she could hear his breath becoming labored. So long...It seemed they would never end it; that they relished every moment they could get out of him. The dogs drew closer, seeming to huddle about him. Flashing their teeth and growling.

None so far had bitten him. They didn't need to. Jessie could see for herself that he wouldn't be able to keep it up much longer. But, she stood by the door, frozen and powerless to help.

If the dogs had seen her they didn't seem to notice. If they had she would've closed the door, and Lance might not have overcome the terror that had until then, held him back.

Her thoughts had been for her horse; not the young pup that suddenly charged to his rescue. She screamed his name once...and when she did the pack noticed her.

16
From the Heart

Ponies can be quick but, at the pace they had gone, Prince wouldn't be able to return home. The dogs had chased them down the road in front of the old house and in the opposite direction.

In tandem the boys headed their mounts toward the Double D. Prince's flank had been slashed in the pursuit and it had him racing on in pure fright.

Almost two miles after the chase had began, they had finally pulled far enough away from the dogs that the pack had given up and lay panting on the road. They had lost prey before and had not found it necessary to wind themselves for it.

Robert MacMurray was in the pasture saddling up is gelding when the boys rode in. It was dumb luck that made him forget his list of appointments and had made him turn back for home. When he found Sky and Jessie gone he had been furious and worried at the same time. There had been another killing and this one was close by the ranch.

His horse lifted his head and Robert stopped his work to watch the boys galloping towards him. They appeared past endurance and he knew that they wouldn't be without valid reason.

King skidded to a stop at the gate, followed in short order by the pinto, and Adam stuttered out the nightmare; if not for the whinnying of their horses the two of them might really have been killed.

That settled it once and for all in Robert's mind. When the pack turned on human beings there was no choice than to hunt them down with every man he could muster.

His call went first to the Sheriff. After he told him the story he called two of the men who had been tracking the dogs with him. He left orders to round up more men; carefully adding that his daughter was alone and on her way to the old farmhouse.

Adam only listened to first call and nodded to Joey to follow him back outside. "I'm going back with him."

"You can't," Joey said. "King is done upon and I can't ask Prince to go again. He's lame."

"Mr. McMurray can take his truck," Adam answered, untying the gelding and climbing into the tall saddle. "He won't need his Horse. We know where the dogs are."

Joey kept silent as his friend rode away. He knew Adam wouldn't stay and argue and he made more use of his time walking the heat out of his horses.

At first the old horse kept a good pace. Adam had no intention of pushing him. He'd need the animals' strength if he came upon the pack again. Even so the horse seemed tired long before it came in site of the house.

Before he arrived he pulled up well short, searching the land and listening. What he heard was Sky's hoof beats shortly before Jessie burst from the trees. She had taken the long way about, not knowing the roadside path had been cleared. His view from down the road still left him a far clip from the house and he nudged the horse into a slow canter.

She was entering the house when he came into view of the front of it. It was then that the dogs came out of the woods and, he didn't dare to call out to her. The horse beneath him panicked when Sky blew out his first terrified whinny and it was all Adam could do to control him. As he did he heard Sky sending out his distress and finally Jessie's voice screaming out for her pup.

He dragged the gelding to a halt and dropping to the ground, uncinched the heavy saddle. Flinging himself on to the bareback he whistled for all he was worth. Digging his heels into the sides of the old horse he forced him towards the house. It worked.

The dogs stopped mauling the pup and, by mutual consent, they launched themselves towards him. There would be no quick getaway now. His only hope was that Jessie's dad would meet him somewhere down the road.

The horse whirled about and was ready for flight but, he held him to a fast canter; desperately trying to save him for the race that was sure to come.

Tears blurred Jessie's vision as she knelt at the still form of Lancelot lying on the ground. He was bleeding from cuts that seemed to cover his entire body.

He didn't stir as she picked him up and carried him to the still restive colt. Holding his weight against hers she snatched the reigns from the tree. Sky had nearly pulled himself free and they came away loosely.

Choking back her tears she walked him over to the porch and gently gained his back. Laying Lance across the saddle in front of her and holding him with one hand she sent Sky off towards home.

She followed the trail that had taken her there; afraid to follow the same path the dogs had. Cantering slowly under the canopy of the trees; the beauty and peace of the woods made even more ugly the poor dog in her lap. She seemed out for a nice ride but for that.

Adam had let the black horse have his head far sooner than he would have liked. Still more than half a mile from the ranch, the road curved lonely in front of him.

The dogs were still fit enough to bark at him when his horse began to stumble. He had managed to keep a good distance ahead until then and had kept the horse from going faster. If he kept the distance between them short they might not give up; as they had before; and head back to Jessie and her exhausted colt. They wouldn't stand a second attack and he had seen for himself that the dogs had gained fight with Skys' prolonged resistance to them.

But, now as they closed in; and the gelding began to falter; he did what he swore he would never do to a horse. He dug his heels and in the black sides and worked the loose ends of the reigns back and forth across its' shoulders like whips.

"Come on! Ya!" he shouted; his hands and feet working feverishly on the sweat drenched coat.

A few yards were gained and he eased off his abuse. The toll it had taken came with the ragged sucking sounds coming with every breath the old horse took. It wouldn't work a second time.

They were at his heels when the truck pulled out onto the road. Not barking anymore but, lunging at the horses' flanks.

The first shots rang out as he lurched past the blue pickup and a large brown mongrel flipped over into its side, rolling as if pitched. Adam circled the uncaring horse around the truck and jumped from its back as two more volleys from the gun crushed another.

As Adam wrenched the door open and clambered inside the weight of another, gone mad animal; threw itself against it and slammed it behind him.

Another car drove up beside them and three men opened fire on the outlaws. Adam put his head down on his chest and held his hands over his ears, as the last of the pack met its end. This time the dogs never had a chance to run.

17

If You Love Them

essie wasn't crying when she entered the yard and turned Sky loose. There was no room in her mind for anything except the determination she had to save her animals. She was nearly running toward the house when she spotted that Debby's car was home.

She kicked at the kitchen door hopping from foot to foot as she did, until Debby answered it. She rushed through as Debby held it back for her and headed straight for the clinic.

Laying him down on the table she began to methodically collect the things they would need. It was like she'd done a hundred times before but, this time she was not going to leave!

Together they cleaned his wounds and began the healing that until then she had sworn she would never do. If it meant saving him, she would gladly bear it all. For the first time she understood the enormity of her fathers' work. Slowly she and Debby patched his wounds and gave him the medicine he needed. He was awake and he knew she was there with him the whole time.

Lance lay on a rug in front of the fire bandaged so completely that it seemed he might not feel the heat coming from it. Ever so often he would shiver and his young owner would rub his head lovingly. His tail would thump the floor and he would be still again.

Adam had told Robert what had happened at the old house and after they had made a search of the place he had returned home quickly to help his daughter with her dog. The other farmers were more than glad to dispose of the menace that had plagued them.

"They were probably good dogs once. It's horrid how they had to meet their end," Robert said suddenly. "It's not an excuse for what they had become but, once in their lives they might have lain just like him." He nodded at Lance who was watching him talk. The pup whined and rolled his eyes back over towards his mistress.

"Then why didn't their owners keep them?" Adam asked. "What would make people dump their dogs off out here?"

"Ignorance," Max answered, cursing. "Ignorance and heartlessness."

"Not only that," Claudia continued. "I think it happens when people throw something away. You don't see it any more so it must be okay."

The men in the room heartily agreed with that; fuming about their losses.

"Well, I hope I never have to deal with it again myself," Sheriff Hill said.

"Not much chance of that," Claudia said. "But, as long as there are people that discard their dogs and cats, to suffering by themselves, there is that chance," said Debby, testily. "And still all we can do is wait and see. It might be years or never."

Jessie had sat stroking her pup all the while they talked and hadn't said a word. He would be all right. They had done their best.

Dads' gelding had died. The strain was too much for him. He'd saved her life. He'd brought Adam back in safe and they couldn't save him.

Sky was young and would recover. He'd let Lance on his back with no fear of him. Prince was stitched and resting in a stall, lame but it wouldn't last long. King, pleasing himself to munch up all the lawn they had, showed the wear he'd taken by favoring one of his legs and nothing else.

She smiled of a sudden and looked at her father with shining eyes. "I'm just glad our job is to be there for them, when they need us, as they are when we need them," she said softly.

The End